"Weird, dark, funny, and original. Amy M. Vaughn delivers the freaky goods."   —Danger Slater, author of *Impossible James*

"*Freak Night at the Slee-Z Motel* is a super fun read! Highly recommended!"
     —Carlton Mellick III, author of *The Terrible Thing That Happens*

"Brutal, heartbreaking and hilarious. This book has it all. Vaughn is a writer to be reckoned with."
               —Gina Ranalli, author of *Swarm of Flying Eyeballs*

"A fast-paced, action-packed descent into macabre madness. Vaughn is one of the best of the new breed of horror writers."
               —Adam Millard, author of *The Bad Game* and *Larry*

"Amy Vaughn's tight prose hurtles you into a whirlwind of circus freaks and other crazy characters. This maniacally violent bizarro romp is tense and tough but still manages to be a ton of fun."
                 —Betty Rocksteady, author of *The Writhing Skies*

FREAK NIGHT AT THE SLEE-Z MOTEL

Amy M. Vaughn

THICKE & VANEY BOOKS
CATLETT, VA

FREAK NIGHT AT THE SLEE-Z MOTEL
Copyright © 2020 by Amy M. Vaughn

ISBN: 978-1-7348324-1-9

First paperback edition published by Thicke & Vaney Books
October 2020

thickeandvaney.us

Cover Design by Ira Rat
Typeset by Michael Kazepis

Thicke & Vaney Books
P O Box 223
Catlett, VA 20119

CHAPTER 1
IN THE VAN

The van and its gypsy-caravan-painted trailer barreled west on the desert highway. Faster vehicles appeared in the rearview, passed on the left, and disappeared into the horizon.

Scrolled along the side of the van in an Old English font were the words "Main Event Sideshow." And inside the van were the players, the working stiffs, of this particular troupe, who hours before had wrapped up another gig, another wild party, and were now on their way to the next one.

On the bench seat, the two newest additions to the group, Jacquelyn and Madelyn Bunker, sat next to Hannah, the Headless Lady. Shiva, the Fire Eater, was driving—two hands on the wheel and two smaller hands holding his cup of coffee. Next to him, DJ Dogface, eyes closed and mouth open, drooled into the curly black hair that covered his face as well as every other inch of his skin. And behind them all, filling her cushioned platform, rode Kitten Dumptruck: owner, mind reader, and resident Fat Lady.

Madelyn—Maddie—slept, resting her head on her sister's shoulder. Jackie gazed out the window, forehead to the glass, drifting in and out of consciousness. She wore a small smile on her face. The night before had been the twins' first performance with the freak show.

CHAPTER 2
BEFORE THE VAN

It was raining, so the sisters were huddled together under an umbrella. Their gait had fallen into that syncopated rhythm the way twins' gaits will: inner legs, outer legs, inner legs, outer legs.

Across the street from campus they had to stop for a traffic light, and that's where Jackie saw the flyer, bright orange even in the gray drizzle. A NIGHT LIKE NO OTHER, it said. FEATURING DJ DOGFACE AND THE MAIN EVENT SIDESHOW. She wanted to go. She needed to go. She knew spontaneously deep in her soul that she *had* to go to this. The trick would be getting Maddie to say yes.

Because Maddie said no to everything. Maddie was always a buzzkill. Sure, in retrospect, she'd probably been right about some things—most recently she'd been right about not going to that frat party where every girl in the room had been dosed with rohypnol. But Maddie never wanted to do anything fun, even if it was harmless. No movies, no concerts, no nothing. She said she felt like everyone, like *every single person*, was either staring at them or trying hard *not* to stare at them.

Jackie used to think Maddie said no to everything because she was weak. But recently she'd realized it wasn't weakness.

Maddie was strong, and she used that strength to dig her heels in.

Jackie ripped the soggy flyer off its pole. "We're going to this," she said, shoving the paper at her sister.

Maddie took a minute to read it. The address was in an industrial part of town. The hours were ridiculously late at night. Besides DJ Dogface, it promised a psychic Fat Lady, a four-armed Fire Eater, and a Headless Woman. It promised a once-in-a-lifetime night of drinking, dancing, and entertainment. Jackie braced for the fight.

"Alright," Maddie said.

Jackie was stunned into silence. The light turned and Maddie took a step forward, yanking her sister out of her daze.

"Really?" Jackie asked.

"Really," Maddie said. "Maybe we finally won't be the biggest freaks in the room."

Leslie saw the application lying on the front desk and thought, *What the fuck is this?*

"Virginia!" she yelled over her shoulder, toward the manager's apartment just off the motel's tiny reception area. "What the fuck is this?"

"What?"

"This application."

"I put an ad out. I thought you wanted me to," Virginia said, still speaking loudly so Leslie could hear her. "You said so yourself, we're getting too old to run this place on our own."

"I said no such thing."

"You did."

"Well, maybe. But I never meant we should hire some kid. I thought maybe we could just burn the place down."

"Come on now," Virginia said, using her *be reasonable* tone, "what's the worst that could happen?"

Damn if that wasn't just like her, Leslie thought. They weren't getting old. They were middle-aged at worst. Sure, she'd been covering her gray hairs with the same red hair dye for a few years now, but it wasn't like they had liver spots and turkey necks. And maybe it did take a little more effort for her to move the furniture, and maybe she did feel like napping most afternoons, but there was no way in hell she was going to bring another poor schmuck into this rotten business of a motel. Of that she was damn sure.

"So that's pretty much the size and shape of things when it comes to checking people in. You'll be in charge of keeping the courtyard clean, too."

"Yes ma'am."

That's how he was, this Jasper kid. All "yes ma'am," "no ma'am," and "sure thing." His demeanor went with his gangly limbs and his freckles. Leslie was glad that if they did have to bring somebody on, at least he was the type who went along with things, wasn't one to stir the pot. And then—

"I do have one question."

Leslie steeled herself.

"It's just, I heard a rumor that there was some kind of accident or something here a while back. I was just wondering what happened."

"Nothing," she told him. "Nothing is what happened. It was a little electrical fire, that's all."

It certainly wasn't a gruesome horror show leaving half a dozen bodies eviscerated, decapitated, and otherwise dead on the floor. And it had nothing at all to do with her choosing that particular time to completely refurbish the rooms right down to their wallpaper. Nope, just a hair dryer and a coffee maker overloading a circuit.

"Okay then," Leslie continued, giving him the side eye, looking to see if he was going to press the issue. He didn't. "This here's the courtyard. Not having a pool keeps things easy. Mostly you just gotta come out here and scrub the bird shit off the benches and tables in the morning."

"What about that?" The boy pointed toward the well.

Of course he would ask about that, Leslie thought. Damn thing takes up half the courtyard with its pretty little shingled roof and old-timey stonework. Thing's goddamn picturesque. Draws people right in.

Even after they'd posted the signs telling people to keep back, guests would still sneak over for a picture or to drop a quarter down. So they'd surrounded it with a square of "decorative" blue and green crushed and broken glass and used some of the shards to line the rim. "To keep all manner of living things away," Leslie had said.

"That? Son, you stay away from that. There's a giant fucking lizard in that well, and give her half a chance, she'll eat your balls off."

The boy's eyes grew wide.

"Right, let's move on to the rooms. You won't have to do them often, but maybe sometimes, so you ought to know how."

Most nights Jacquelyn and Madelyn Bunker sat on the bed in their tiny dorm room; Maddie with her laptop open, doing homework, and Jackie with her headphones on and her eyes glued to her phone. This night was only different because they both had their screens trained to the same page: the Main Event Sideshow's website.

Jackie took out her earbuds and poked Maddie.

"I want to wear the yellow tank tops," she said.

This was, of course, a loaded statement. The girls looked great in yellow. It was a striking contrast against their already strikingly deep black skin. For the same reason, Jackie wore an ornate gold loop though her septum. But the tank top was a half shirt, which meant blatantly revealing the ligament that connected them—the coffee-can-sized cylinder that started just below their ribs on Jackie's right and Maddie's left side. They had worked hard to stretch it every day of their lives, and now, instead of angling toward each other, they could both face forward.

Back in their little hometown they'd taken dance lessons, and the yellow tank top was part of a recital costume. Back there, everybody knew about their connection and how they shared a circulatory system, which relied on their single beating heart that pumped in Jackie's chest. Back there, life was far from perfect, but at least they had people who knew them and loved them, family and friends who comforted them when other people's idiocy penetrated the girls' feigned indifference about being different.

But things weren't the same in the city. No one here had known them since they were little. No one here was used to seeing two people stuck together.

Since they'd moved, Maddie would only wear clothes that hid their connection. Of course, there was no hiding the existence of it, but their clothes could at least cover the biological flesh of it. And, even more importantly to Maddie, with it under their shared shirts people didn't ask to touch it.

"The yellow tank tops?" Maddie repeated.

"Yes," Jackie said. "I'm not budging."

"With baggy jeans and black Chucks," Maddie said, negotiating. She'd given in easier than Jackie thought she would, but still, Jackie couldn't resist bartering.

"With *skinny* jeans and black *heels*," Jackie countered.

"No way. It's a rave. I'm not dancing in heels all night," Maddie said, putting her foot down. "And we can't be different heights for that long either; our sides would ache for days. So, yellow tanks, skinny jeans, and Chucks."

"Okay," Jackie said.

"Okay," Maddie echoed.

And they went back to their devices and their own individual lives.

Leslie enjoyed cleaning the rooms. She believed there was a certain way things should be and that keeping things tidy kept the chaos away. When Leslie cleaned a room, she was putting that one little part of the world back in order again.

She'd developed this belief in the power of The Way Things Ought To Be when she was very young. She learned it from the kids at school who taunted and laughed at anyone who was ugly or poor or different. She learned it from the reel-to-reel films in health class about how many strokes it took to properly brush your hair and just how to circle your toothbrush to get your teeth their cleanest. She learned it from her mother, who always kept everything in the house just so. And she learned it from her father, who came home late from the bar and broke dishes and split lips if anything was out of place, and he could always find something out of place if he wanted to.

Checkout time was 11:00, and at 11:15 Leslie started with Room 1. It was a good thing there were only ten rooms, she often thought. Otherwise there would never be enough time to get them all done before new guests started to arrive.

She had a routine she followed in every room, every day. The rooms no one stayed in took less time, but still, she did every room, every day. Unless the "Do Not Disturb" sign was out.

Then she tried hard not to imagine what kind of debauchery could be going on just one thin wall away from where she was setting things straight again.

At 11:15, she'd begin the ritual. She didn't move fast, just steadily. First, she took care of any trash. Next she dusted, moving clockwise around the room. She stripped and made the beds. Then she moved on to the bathroom where she would start again, working clockwise, wiping everything down. She'd do the linoleum floor, and then, finally, she would vacuum the main room carpet. She used the outlet by the door so she wouldn't leave even a footprint.

In the empty rooms she might just dust, wipe down the sink, and vacuum, which was the least she felt she could get away with. The desert crept in everywhere.

Leslie found a lot of things frustrating about cleaning the rooms: when people moved the furniture and didn't move it back; when it looked like they'd been messy just for the sake of being messy; and pubic hair—Leslie hated that she had to contend with other people's pubic hair. But worst of all was the late checkout. Not only did it sabotage her routine, but it had been a late checkout that ruined her life, that tied her to the motel, that kept her living in constant fear of being found out.

It had been years since either of the twins felt this free. Under the strobing lights, feeling the pulse of the music and their own heat mixing with that of the blissed-out dancers around them, for long moments each one found herself lost, ecstatic, until a new person would appear and see their uniqueness. And in this magical place where the love drugs flowed, where race and gender disappeared, where the DJ was covered head to toe in luxurious curls, a man with four arms juggled flaming batons, and an acrobat with no head performed high above them—in this place, their deformity never failed to elicit a smile, or a double fist bump, or, from the overly exuberant (often multi-ponytailed) party creatures, an unsolicited though not unwelcome hug.

They were on display in their yellow tank tops. Jackie smiled more than once at her choice. If they'd covered up their connection, people still would have looked, stared, tried to figure out what was up with the sisters who stayed side by side, even in the bathroom. Showing it turned the surreptitious glances and questioning looks into acceptance and admiration, two things Jackie had craved all her life. Maddie too, if she would admit it.

Well into the evening, when the girls were drenched with sweat and shimmering with other people's glitter, when they were deeply entranced—absorbed, transported, and palpitated by the rhythm—the crowd around them parted. Sensing the sudden absence of humanity, they looked to see Kitten Dumptruck lumbering toward them. She relied heavily on two canes, and her giant sequined smock transformed her into a great big disco ball under the pulsing colored lights.

"Come," Kitten bellowed to be heard over the music. And, after a blink-and-you'd-miss-it-quick glance to check in with each other, they followed her.

Kitten led them through the gyrating crowd, away from the stage and the speakers, to the far end of the warehouse where her tent was set up. It was red and white striped with high sides and a peaked top. A sign outside offered "Mind Readings $20." A few people milled around nearby. Some were waiting for Kitten to return. Others were daring each other, or summoning the courage, to talk to her.

When they got to the tent, Kitten flipped the sign so it read "In Session." The three of them entered the small space, and the heavy canvas muffled the music outside. The only light came from a glowing globe on a small table. Surrounding the table were two high-backed chairs and an old brocade loveseat, into which Kitten dropped, filling it from side to side. The twins moved the chairs together and sat down.

"I'd like for you to join us," Kitten said, getting straight to business.

The girls spoke over each other: an excited "Yes!" from Jackie and a dispirited "We can't" from Maddie.

Jackie faced her sister. "Oh *come on*, Maddie, it would be amazing. Look around, we belong here."

"What about school? What about my degree? I can't just quit."

"You hate it there as much as I do. Maddie, please, let's do this!"

Kitten interrupted, "I understand your hesitation. And I'll understand if you can't join us, or if you're not ready. My offer will stand for as long as we're in business. But . . ." Kitten paused here and looked at Maddie. Few people knew Kitten's mind reading only worked with eye contact, but in that moment, Maddie was one of those few. When Kitten spoke again she tread softly, deliberately, the way she always did when she was telling someone their own truth. "You know as well as I do that things rarely go according to plan. For some of us, that's our very first life lesson. Maybe it's time to switch plans, give something new a chance."

Maddie didn't answer right away. Jackie bounced in her seat with excitement. Under her breath, and smacking her sister on the thigh, Maddie said, "Knock it off. I can't think with you shaking me around."

She looked back at Kitten, expecting her to say more, but the Fat Lady had said her piece and seemed content to wait for Maddie to make up her mind. She turned toward her sister, who was sitting still now, with her hands clenched together in her lap and her eyebrows halfway up her forehead.

Maddie sighed. "Fuck it," she said, and Jackie let out the breath she'd been holding. "Might as well get paid to be who we are."

"Thank you thank you thank you!" Jackie said. She pecked her sister on the cheek.

"Well," Kitten said, "there's a little bit more to it than that."

The twins tensed, ready for the catch.

Kitten went on, "Everyone in the show has to have a 'working act.' In some states, exhibiting a living human being for money is illegal. So every one of us here in the freak show has to have a talent, a job title like 'Fire Eater' or 'Blockhead.' You probably already have some talent that might fit the bill."

The last statement was really a question, but Jackie and Maddie were both too hung up to answer. Since Kitten had said the word "freak" they'd been awash with discomfort. Dark memories of shame and embarrassment climbed up from the flesh they shared and brought to mind every instance of fear they had ever been through, every occasion of discrimination, every time anyone had made them feel wrong for being who and what they were.

Out of all the possible memories, both twins' minds settled on the same one: the time at the pool when they were seven years old. The time when they had started out happy in their new yellow-and-white-flowered two-piece swimsuits. The time when Jimmy Johnson's little cousin from two towns over, who had never seen them before and hadn't been warned, had pointed at them as they stood there on the side of the pool, before they'd even gotten wet—pointed at them and screamed. And he just kept screaming, until all the babies in the wading pool were crying, until every head in the mid-June public swimming pool had swiveled their direction.

"Maybe I don't want to be in a freak show," Jackie said.

Maddie sat taller, pulling her sister up with her. "You're going to be scared off by a word? If that word belongs to anybody, it belongs to us."

The McCrorys, who had owned the Wishing Well Motel, were never able to have children of their own. Leslie started working for them when she was sixteen, and before long they thought of her as the daughter they never had. So when Mrs. McCrory found the girl huddled, crying, between the dryer and the shelves of clean, folded linen, she got right down there on the floor and asked, "What is it, sweetheart? What's the matter?"

Leslie could hardly get the truth out between her sobs, but when she finally did, Mrs. McCrory didn't hesitate, didn't even think, before saying, "Don't you worry. You'll just move in here with us."

Leslie knew it wasn't exactly The Way Things Ought To Be, but nothing was going to be exactly the way it ought to be ever again, and this was at least *an answer* to what she thought was an unsolvable problem. She couldn't have an abortion. That was the most wrong of all the wrong options. She couldn't live in town, in her father's house; she couldn't even tell her father. She couldn't leave; she didn't have anywhere to go. So, she slept on the McCrorys' fold-out couch in the cramped little manager's apartment behind the office, and she kept cleaning the rooms, defending at least those ten little boxed-up parts of the world from disintegrating into chaos every day. In time, she learned how to run the front desk and how to do the nightly audit. The McCrorys were good to her. They were kind people by nature, and they kept paying her wages while giving her free room and board.

The little girl was born at the motel one sweltering August night. She wasn't perfect—her fingers and toes were webbed—but the McCrorys took to her instantly. They called her Wendy and coddled and cooed at her. It took Leslie a little longer to get over the baby's disfigured hands and feet. She thought maybe this deformity was even more punishment for having had sex out of wedlock, for that one-afternoon-stand with a late checkout. But after a few weeks, something switched off in Leslie's mind, and she began to simply ignore the webbing, pretend it didn't exist.

Life went on. Mr. McCrory taught Leslie how to keep the monthly books, how to shoot the revolver he kept under the front counter in case of thieves, and how to drive his three-gear pickup truck.

"We're old," he said. "We're gonna have to retire one of these days, and when we do, you'll need to know how to do all this stuff."

Leslie didn't take him seriously. She had an infant to deal with and no savings. She would never be able to buy the motel from them. Humoring him, she said, "That's not for a good long while yet."

She didn't know he'd willed the Wishing Well to her.

Time moved along like lightning and at a snail's pace, the way it will with a little one around. And besides the baby growing into a toddler, nothing really changed around the motel. That is, nothing changed until one morning when Leslie eased her way to sitting on the side of the hide-a-bed and looked into the playpen where the little girl, now somewhere between three and four years old, lay sprawled out, breathing softly in her sleep. Her one stuffed animal, a little white lamb, spilled out from her open hand.

At first, Leslie couldn't comprehend what she was seeing. Instead of the smooth baby skin she should have had, the toddler was covered with scales. More than anything else, it reminded Leslie of the parched and crusty hexagons on a dry salt flat.

It's possible this change had been progressing slowly for a long time and Leslie had simply been ignoring it, suppressing it, just like she suppressed the girl's little webbed fingers and toes; just like she suppressed the shame she felt at being an unwed mother, the embarrassment that led her to keep her pregnancy quiet and her child a secret; just like she suppressed her disappointment and heartbreak and anger every day she led this life that didn't in any way resemble the one she wanted for herself. Yes, denial was a definite possibility.

As she looked into that playpen and acknowledged her daughter's scales for the first time, all those wrong things in her life, all that chaos that had been churning just below the surface, broke through.

Leslie snapped.

She picked up the little monster, tucked it under one arm, and marched outside. She went to the well and pitched it in without looking down to see what had become of it.

When Leslie got back to the office, Mrs. McCrory asked her, "Where's Wendy?" And that's when Leslie took the gun from under the counter and shot Mrs. McCrory through the head. Three seconds later, when Mr. McCrory appeared in the doorway, she shot him too. The bodies were just feet from each other. She set the scene to look like a murder-suicide, the way she'd hoped to find her parents so many times before.

Working quickly, Leslie gathered any evidence that a child had ever lived there, bagged it up and heaved it into the back of Mr. McCrory's pickup truck. She drove out to the middle of the desert and dumped it there.

When she got back, she started to pick up the phone, but she heard a sound that made her wait. Before she could call the police, she'd have to do something about the crying coming from the well.

It was a muggy Saturday night in El Paso. The music was loud, the warehouse was packed, and Jackie was happier than she could ever remember being. Shiva's flashy fire eating was to the right of DJ Dogface's command center, and the twins were to the left. They wore shiny red leotards with sequined holes in the side for their connection, Jackie's on her right and Maddie's on her left.

Up on the stage, Dogface faded into a new track, and as the music ramped up, the girls stood facing the crowd, the shaft of flesh that bound them shining like the rest of their onyx skin under the bright lights. They lifted their arms and leaned back, arching their spines and lowering their hands to the floor behind them. They paused here, their own double rainbow, and adjusted their hands so their fingers pointed toward their heels.

With coordinated deliberation, Jackie and Maddie picked up their right hands and stepped them toward their feet. Then they did the same with their left, then right, then left. Until finally each girl's hands were beside her feet, their heads were between their shins, and their faces smiled out at the crowd. Their backs were bent completely in half. The twins held the pose while the music swelled and the crowd around them buzzed and crackled with increasing energy. Finally, they unfolded from their backbend and danced, arms lifted, hips keeping time with the deep, steady bass.

Using their natural gifts of coordination and flexibility as go-go dancers / contortionists for their working act was only the beginning. Kitten had encouraged them to strive for something with more wow factor, something more shocking. So Jackie was learning to be a Human Pincushion from Shiva, who knew all about everything sideshow. She could already run a sewing needle through one cheek and out the other with minimal bleeding. Maddie, for her part, was picking up the art of knife throwing. At first she was too timid, too worried about rotation and arc, and wasn't using enough force to get them to stick. But once Kitten gave her a special set, smooth and sleek, made of perfectly black steel, she got the hang of it and found she thrilled at her own controlled strength as she got closer to her targets.

But for now, they danced. From up on the stage they could see everything.

They could see DJ Dogface bobbing his head and twisting his dials, and the girl under the table who had just sucked him off and had a mouthful of hair for her troubles.

They could see Shiva whooshing all four of his fire fans in time with the beat, the flask of paraffin he'd use for his Dragon's Breath grand finale already on stage at his feet.

They could see Hannah, the Headless Lady, up on the high wire, riding her unicycle and juggling. Sometimes she juggled machetes, sometimes chainsaws. Right now it was water balloons, which she would purposefully let drop onto the overheated dancers beneath her.

The twins could see Kitten's little red-and-white-striped tent in the back of the warehouse, with a short line of people waiting to get their minds read.

But mostly they could see the crowd, the sea of people nodding their heads, pumping their fists, pogoing, pulsating, and smiling so big their faces would ache the next day.

The twins smiled too. Jackie closed her eyes and let the music sweep her away. After a bit—could have been two minutes, could have been ten—Maddie nudged her. Jackie opened her eyes and saw why. Kitten was standing just outside the entrance to her tent, leaning all of her six-hundred-plus pounds on her canes, and she was looking right at them. It was time to earn their keep.

They dove into a four-handed handstand, twisted their inner legs together and rotated their outer legs around in half splits. It was a graceful movement, like synchronized swimming, even if the twins were feeling a little less like fish out of water.

CHAPTER 3
BACK TO THE VAN

"Holy shit!" Shiva said, grabbing the wheel with all four hands and breaking the road-weary silence in the van.

Next to him, Dogface sat up and wiped the spittle from the corners of his mouth. With his hand still raised to his face, he said it too, "Holy shit."

"Right?" Shiva said. "You ever seen anything like it?"

Further back, the women were waking up and seeing for themselves the enormous wall of dust barreling toward them. It spanned the horizon as far north and south as they could see. Headless Hannah reached forward and placed her hand on Shiva's shoulder.

"Gee-zuz," Jackie said. "That thing has to be thirty stories tall."

"What do we do?" Maddie asked.

From the back of the van, Kitten's voice rang clear, "It's a haboob, a giant sandstorm kicked up by a cold front. It'll be impossible to drive through. We can either pull over and sit it out or find somewhere to crash for the night. I, for one, would rather sleep in a bed. Phoenix can wait."

There was a hubbub of general agreement.

"Thank fuck," Dogface said, lifting his hips to fish his phone out of his pocket. "Road dreams are fucked up." He swiped his finger across the screen, ready to find them a hotel. After a few seconds of nothing happening, he held the phone up toward the windshield and squinted at it. "No signal."

Everyone else checked their phones, too.

"Do you think it's the storm?" Maddie asked.

"It's probably because there are no frickin' towers out here in Bumfuck fucking Egypt," Dogface said.

"Alright," Kitten said. "Just stop at the first place you can find."

Shiva stepped on the gas, taking the jittering van and its trailer past seventy, seventy-five, eighty, to cover as much ground as possible, to give them their best shot at finding shelter before the vast wall of sand engulfed them.

Every member of the Main Event Sideshow leaned forward in their seats and scanned the flat, brown horizon, willing a motel to appear. Preferably one with new mattresses and plenty of hot water. As the miles of asphalt disappeared behind them, the van developed worrying new squeals and clanks. The mammoth cloud of dirt grew taller, soaring up into the sky, and the wind grew stronger. Tiny pieces of sand and larger chunks of road and desert debris tinked and scratched at the windows. The van rocked violently with each gust, sending the frightened freaks straining against their seatbelts. More than once they watched the trailer go up on two wheels. Shiva had to slow down.

"There! There! There!" It was Dogface who saw it. "Fucking two o'clock." He pointed off to the right. But the dust storm consumed whatever he had seen before anybody else could spot it.

"Good enough for me," Shiva said, as he continued to decrease their speed to fifteen, ten, five miles an hour. The air had grown thick and brown. Visibility was down to a few feet at best. Shiva hugged the white line and followed it up an exit.

"Left or right?" he said when they got to the frontage road.

"Left," Dogface said. "I think."

He made the turn and they crawled along through the dirty fog until the asphalt opened up to the right. Guessing, Shiva steered them into what he hoped was a parking lot.

As they crept forward, a sign emerged out of the gritty mist. It was shaped like an old-fashioned wishing well and said "SLEEP E-Z MOTEL." On either side of it were large posts that presumably went up to a much bigger sign that would normally be seen from the highway but was now completely obscured in the storm.

"There," Dogface said, pointing. The outline of a building was coming into view. Shiva eased the van toward it. They came to a wall upon which, luckily, was painted the word "office" and an arrow pointing to the right. He put their traveling behemoth in park and turned off the engine. All six members of the Main Event Sideshow took a deep breath and sat back in their seats.

Shiva slid his smaller arms into the sleeves of his jacket. He hated to do it. Hiding his supernumerary limbs reminded him of his childhood. But even with his olive skin, Shiva was the most able to pass, to look "normal," and got these kinds of tasks by default. What he hated even more was having to use his given name to secure the rooms. He was Shiva now, and Anton felt like a bad dream from long ago.

"Back in a minute," he said.

As he reached for the door handle, he felt Hannah's hand on his shoulder. He turned toward her. She took one of his hands in both of hers and squeezed it.

"Don't worry," he said. "It's just another crappy roadside motel."

Shiva shrugged his jacket up to cover his nose and mouth and leapt from the van. He ran to the office door and pulled against the wind, opening it just enough to squeeze through. The door slammed closed behind him and the bells on the interior handle jangled.

"Just a minute." The words came from behind the chest-high front desk.

Shiva shook the sand from his hair and stepped toward the counter. On the other side, a puff of brown curls, streaked heavily with gray, hovered close to a crossword puzzle. The woman finished entering letters into boxes and stood up.

"Well," she said, "aren't you a handsome one!"

He was used to this. Women of a "certain age" often found Shiva's chiseled good looks especially appealing. He reminded them of golden age movie stars like Rock Hudson and Montgomery Clift—the ones people called virile. He attributed his looks and his whole tall, strong, masculine physique to having two sets of genitals to go along with his two sets of arms, and the ensuing four balls worth of testosterone.

He was about to start in with his "Aw shucks" routine when the woman went on.

"If I wasn't a lesbian and smack in the middle of menopause, I'd probably be flooding my panties over you. But," she held her hands palms forward at hip height, "dry as that dirt blowing around out there. Now, what can I do ya for?"

Shiva took a moment to compose himself. A quip like that would have been unexpected from anyone, but it was especially at odds with this woman's country-grandmother look.

"Yes. Hi." He smiled, too used to using his charm to forego it. "I need three rooms please. One with two queens, two with kings."

"We don't got queens honey, let alone kings. Every room has two double beds."

The twins would be fine, Shiva figured, but Kitten would likely spill out of a double bed.

"Well, I guess we'll make do. Maybe we could come to some sort of deal, especially since I'm renting multiple rooms?"

"Of course," she said. "The rooms are usually fifty bucks apiece, but for you, I'll give you all three for a hundred and fifty, plus tax." She smiled her grandma smile.

Shiva played along and smiled back.

Minutes later she was handing him the keys to Rooms 2, 3, and 4 and pointing at a little map of the motel. Rooms 2 and 3 were on the same wing as the office, and Room 4 was just after the walkway took a right turn.

"Thanks," Shiva said. "Wish me luck." He gestured out the door.

"Sandstorm should pass soon. I give it another half hour at most. Then the rain will come. Gonna be a doozy."

"Oh yeah?" Shiva supposed she felt it in her bones, or there was a similar storm every seven years, or she had access to some other form of semi-magical old person wisdom.

"Yep. Said so on the TV."

"Alright then," he said, taking another step toward the door. "Oh hey, it's so dark out there we almost missed this place. You might want to turn your sign on."

"Thank you, son. I will take that into consideration," she said in her not quite sincere, not quite sarcastic way.

He headed out into the whirling dirt.

Now that Shiva knew the lay of the land, he moved the van—which had worryingly retained its new squeals and thunks—so he and Dogface could unhook the trailer. While they were at it, the outside lights came on. The men watched as the sign, a duplicate of the one below it, flickered to life. Neon tubing outlined the shape of a well and spelled out SLEEP E-Z MOTEL, but just for a moment. Then the "P" and the third "E" blinked out, leaving it to say "SLEE - Z MOTEL" instead.

Leaving the trailer alongside the front of the building, next to the office, Shiva goaded the van into one of the parking spaces between the U-shaped motel and its courtyard, the one right outside Room 4. They all pitched in to get Kitten disembarked, the flying dirt grating at them all the while. Then they hustled to their rooms. Jackie, Maddie, and Dogface were sharing Room 2; Hannah and Shiva were in Room 3; and Kitten chose Room 4. It was the best choice, Shiva agreed, away from Dogface who always had either music or the TV on, and away from himself and Headless Hannah, who would be making rhythmic noises of their own.

Kitten sat on the side of the bed feeling the sharp edge of the mattress dig into the backs of her knees. A double bed. This was not luxury. They could have afforded better, but "any port in a storm," she told herself. Maybe she'd ask the guys to push the beds together.

It wasn't the worst place she'd stayed. It looked like a hundred other out-of-date rooms she'd been in: thin caramel-colored carpet liberally splotched with mystery stains; a cathode ray television bolted to the particleboard dresser, which matched the brick-sized remote bolted to the particleboard nightstand; and garishly colored comforters with pegged corners that would be itchy and silky at the same time, like hair from a clogged shower drain.

And the shower, pfft. That tiny stall was useless to her, but at least she could fit through the bathroom door if she turned sideways.

And it didn't stink. Motels like this anywhere else in the country always had that moldy smell that made her feel like she was sleeping in a used towel bin.

Yes, it could have been worse. They could still be in the van.

Kitten used the strength of her arms to heave first one leg and then the other onto the bed. She fit, barely. With the two thin pillows folded in half to support her head and shoulders, she settled in to get some rest.

He meant it innocently enough. He had no way of knowing the stress of adjusting to a new way of life and all those hours on the road had been coming to a head since early that morning. He didn't mean to incite an explosion, but he did.

"You guys want the bed by the door or the one by the bathroom?" Dogface asked.

The twins spoke over each other: Jackie said, "The door," and Maddie said, "The bathroom."

"Jesus Christ, Maddie. You're such a fucking wuss," Jackie said. "What is it? Are you afraid someone's going to come in through the window?"

"What? No. It's because I don't want to sleep six inches from that ancient air conditioning unit that's going to be turning off and on all night. That's just like you," Maddie went on, "jumping to conclusions all the time."

"I do not."

"You do too. You know it. You're too impulsive."

"I'm not too impulsive. You're too cautious."

Dogface backed away and closed himself in the bathroom. He could still hear them through the hollow door, but at least this way he wouldn't be dragged into their fight.

"Maybe I do err on the side of caution," Maddie said, "but it's only because I have to protect myself from your stupid rash decisions."

"Bullshit. I'm the one who has to protect you! What have I ever done that you've had to pay for?"

"How about every time you're around pizza you eat it, even though we're lactose intolerant."

"I do not."

"Yes you do. Or the way you assume the worst about people and get angry at them when they haven't even done anything wrong? Like Tonya? Oh, remember that? When your hot head put us on the outs with the only decent hairdresser in town? And because of what? Because of nothing."

"She might not have said anything, but I saw her thinking it."

"See what I'm saying? And," Maddie's voice got quieter, "what about Christopher?"

Jackie didn't reply right away, and when she did, she said, "Fine. We don't have to sleep next to the air conditioner."

Dogface flushed and came out of the bathroom.

"Bad news," he said. "Shower's a stall."

"Aw shit," the twins said together.

Shiva and Hannah were already naked under the covers and finished with round one by the time the dust started to settle and the first raindrops fell.

People often questioned Shiva about whether he and Hannah had a real relationship. Of course, freak show couples have always fallen under intense scrutiny, ever since Barnum and his kind cashed in on the spectacular weddings between the Skeleton Man and the Fat Lady, between Tom Thumb and little Lavinia Warren, and between the microcephalic Aztec children (two so-called pinheads who had previously been billed as brother and sister). Nobody knew this better than Shiva. But Shiva and Hannah were not together for show.

Shiva loved everything about Hannah. He loved her strength and her forthrightness. He loved her compassion and her patience. He loved her body. And, if he was being really honest, he loved being with an indisputable icon of the freak show. No one else in the world had a pedigree like Hannah. She was fourth-generation sideshow royalty.

Shiva had discovered that there were many benefits to being with a Headless Lady. One of the minor ones was that, as they spooned in the small, lumpy motel bed, he wasn't getting hair up his nose.

As perfect as their relationship felt to him, Shiva still worried that maybe he wasn't enough for her, that maybe she would leave him. Even with his good looks and his charisma, Shiva had deep scars from growing up a freak.

He pulled Hannah closer, wrapping her up in his many arms. She held his tiny hands in hers, and Shiva sighed contentedly.

At least for now, they were sideshow royalty together.

"Why'd you give rooms to those freaks?" Leslie asked Virginia, setting down her plastic tumbler of iced tea.

"Well I didn't know they were freaks when I gave them the rooms, did I now? All I knew was that we run a motel and a nice young man was giving me money, so renting him some rooms seemed the logical next step." Virginia laid her knife and fork on her plate next to the half-finished meatloaf. It was on the dry side, that's how Leslie preferred it.

"Don't be like that," Leslie said. "You've got that look like we're some old married couple getting ready for bickering."

"Well, aren't we? Or the closest thing to it without paperwork?"

"Living together doesn't make us . . ." Leslie paused here, having trouble saying the word, "lesbians."

"No," Virginia said, "I thought the sex part and the giving a shit about each other was what did that."

"I am not gay," Leslie stated. "We've been over this. You and me may be *close*, but we are not a couple. And if you think otherwise, you've been living under a delusion for a dozen years now. Gay ain't no different than those freaks running around out there. Just goes against the natural order. It's not The Way Things Ought to Be."

Virginia closed her mouth, which had been hanging open. She looked from one corner of the room to the other, as if something in their small, overly ornamented kitchen could help her make sense of Leslie's words. True, they weren't a romantic couple; they didn't talk about their relationship much, or ever. But they'd shared a bed for more than a decade. Virginia was pretty sure she wasn't the delusional one.

"'Course that don't mean anything's got to change," Leslie went on. "Good to clear the air though, get on the same page." She dunked a bite of gray meatloaf in ketchup and popped it in her mouth. "Bad enough we gotta house blacks and browns and yellows when they come around, and those damn drunk Indians. No way am I going to abide having freaks under my roof."

"What are you going to do, kick them out into this storm?"

"No, Ginny, that's not what I had in mind."

CHAPTER 4
IN THE ATTIC

The creature imagined the scene through the eye of a camera—webbed fingers gripped the roughhewn stones of the well. Pulling itself up, coarse scales sloughed off in the darkness and floated down onto the piles of discarded skin below. Vaulting onto the rim of the well, lizard's feet careful of the glass set into the cement, glass chipped off and smoothed down years before but that could still deliver a nasty gash with a misstep. For an instant the hunched figure was illuminated by a flash of lightning: it was humanoid, female, naked, and hairless.

Moving gingerly out from under the well's small roof and into the pouring rain, she set one foot and then the other straight down onto the broken glass meant to keep her prisoner. Taking the shortest possible route to the edge, she continued to lift each foot and set it down flat, distributing her weight evenly and giving the glass time to shift and settle beneath her.

Upon reaching the asphalt, the creature forgot about the imaginary film crew and scurried to the rotting trellis at the end of the motel opposite the office. She moved quickly, not wanting anyone to see her, never forgetting—though a long, long time had passed—the noise, the screaming, the fear she'd felt on the night she had been seen.

Later, when the lights were all out, she would test the car doors, scavenge through the garbage for food. Maybe there would be more than just the greasy ends of potato chip bags, the unwanted pickles and tomatoes in paper wrappers that smelled of something so much better than what they contained. But for now, she climbed the trellis and ducked inside the crawlspace above the rooms through a large vent, which she popped out and replaced with well-practiced ease.

Inside the ceiling, the creature gripped the main crossbeam with her webbed fingers and toes. She paused for a moment to savor being out of the rain until the call of a nearby television beckoned her on. Making her way along the beam like a lizard—opposite hand and foot moving simultaneously—she came to the closest ray of light coming up from a room below.

Every room had a vent left over from the old swamp cooler system, replaced decades ago by single unit air conditioners. The ductwork had been removed, but the holes in the ceiling were never covered over. From one angle, the vents gave her a clear view of the television in each room, as well as of the ends of the beds. From the opposite angle, she could see the heads of the beds and usually the room's occupants, but they didn't interest her as much as they used to. She'd spent so many nights in the attic that "the guests," as the old ladies called them, had all become the same.

Below the first vent, in the room with a 10 on the door, she saw a man with pasty skin and a crew cut sitting on the edge of the bed nearest the bathroom. He was facing the window but looking at the TV. To one side of him was a carefully laid out suit jacket and tie, still knotted, and on the other side was an empty holster. The gun was in his right hand. He looked like what the TV called a "G-man," and the gun looked like what the TV called a "Glock."

The G-man's left arm stretched out to the remote bolted to the nightstand. His index finger pressed the channel up button over and over. Images flashed on the screen. This frustrated the creature in the ceiling. Maybe, she thought, when he finally shot the gun through his head, he'd leave the TV on. She could hope.

Television was the ceiling lizard's only friend. Television taught her language, which she practiced in hushed tones in her home at the bottom of the well. Television taught her about a fantasy world of people and places and products, all things that might as well exist on the moon but that filled her nights with pictures and her days, while she slept, with dreams.

And here was this G-man, mindlessly switching channels, wasting precious late-night movie time. But he had that look about him. She'd seen this play out before. With guns, with pills, with lots of blood in the bathroom. The old ladies complained when it happened.

"Why can't they just do it at home?" the one called Leslie would say. "Do they think this place magically cleans itself?"

Fed up with the G-man's channel surfing, the creature navigated the central beam to the next striated column of light, which was three rooms down, just before the first corner. Room 7. She moved like a giant gecko slinking its way across a twig until she could see that what she heard coming from this room was not the TV but the people lying naked on top of the bed covers.

"We shouldn't have stolen from them," a feminine voice said. "It's bad karma, Rail."

"Don't worry," said a masculine voice. "There's no way they'll know it was us. Anyway, it's hardly enough to worry about."

"It could have been everything they had, man. I just hope you're right about them not knowing it was us. We didn't make it very far before that crazy dust storm kicked up."

"Shit, woman, you gotta stop worrying. Come here. Can't you just enjoy the moment? We've had hot showers for the first time in weeks. Our bellies are full. We're out of the rain. And we're in a real bed. Come on, Ox, you have to admit, this is a good day."

The ceiling lizard heard kissing noises and moved on. Sex was boring to her. She wanted sitcoms and police procedurals, comedies and thrillers—stories to laugh and cry to. She continued along the center beam, above the corner room with its ancient vending machines and ice maker. She made the ninety-degree turn carefully, even though there was no one in the room below. The ceiling planks were old and loud; she didn't want to chance it.

She passed a few more dark rooms. The next one with any light coming from it was the one whose door was marked with a 4, the one just before the next corner. Only the bedside lamp was lit. The creature in the attic couldn't see anything except for feet that looked like inflated balloons and cankles that might have been the lower half of a peach- and red-splotched snow suit.

She crawled on, turning the corner over the laundry room, less careful now with the noise from the banging machinery to mask her presence.

But again, at Room 3, no TV. Just two people lying quietly on the bed. She'd gone just beyond the vent when she heard a man's voice say, "What is it, babe? Something in the ceiling?"

The scaly voyeur adjusted her angle so she could see into the room. She was stunned by what she saw—a female figure with no head holding up a bedsheet to cover her breasts with one hand and pointing directly at her with the other.

"Okay," the man said, "I'll check it out." He started to stand up on the bed, to look in the vent. The lizard creature panicked. No one had ever heard her before. She moved fast. Clinging to the center beam, she flung herself forward, out of view. By the time she was above the next room, she was losing her balance. Just a few feet past the dividing wall, she fell hard to her right and crashed through the ceiling, taking large chunks of wood and plaster down with her.

She landed in between two identical young women. Blood pooled quickly on the bed beneath her.

Hannah threw on her clothes and Shiva pulled up his jeans, not bothering to fasten the button or belt. They raced next door and charged into the room.

The scene was chaos. Jackie was screaming, watching blood spurt out of her side where she had been disconnected from her sister. Maddie's lifeless body lay next to her. Between them was a mess of tan wood and white plaster, turning red. A naked woman covered in scales crouched in the corner. She had blood on her back and on her hands. Dogface had the room phone up to his ear.

"No dial tone," he said as Hannah grabbed a pillow and placed it against Jackie's bleeding side. She positioned Jackie's hands so they would hold the pillow in place, and then went across the room to get the iron out of the shallow closet. She brought it back and plugged it into the socket between the beds.

"Did you try dialing 0 or 9?" Shiva asked loudly to be heard over Jackie's screams, which were turning to wails.

Hannah turned the iron up as high as it would go.

Dogface punched the numbers on the phone. "Nothing," he said. "The thing's dead."

Jackie sobbed loudly at the word "dead."

Hannah grabbed Dogface by the shoulders and moved him out of the way. She stripped the top sheet from the bed by the air conditioner and brought it over to Shiva, where she mimed ripping the sheet in half and held it up to his mouth. He bit the material to start a tear and together they created long strips to use as bandages for Jackie.

"It was an accident," the Lizard Woman said. "I fell. It was an accident."

Shiva and Dogface looked at the woman and then at Hannah, whose shoulders lifted and lowered in her version of a sigh. She held up an index finger as if to say, "First things first," then she whipped Shiva's belt from his pants, folded it, and shoved it in Jackie's mouth. Jackie continued to sob deep in her throat.

Hannah picked up the iron.

Shiva saw what she was planning to do and said, "Dogface, help me hold her." Shiva pressed down on Jackie's shoulders. Looking right into her screaming eyes, he told her, "You're going to make it through this." Dogface took hold of her legs.

Hannah leaned over Jackie and pressed the searing hot iron to the wound in her side. Jackie's sobs would have turned back into screams if not for Shiva's belt between her teeth. Smoke rose from the contact and the room filled with the smell of burning flesh. Jackie fought to get away, but Shiva and Dogface held tight.

When it was done—the iron removed and the blood flow staunched—the men backed away and Jackie stopped screaming. She collapsed on the bed with her sister. The belt fell from her mouth, still connected to her by a string of saliva.

Hannah put the makeshift bandages in Shiva's hands and pointed at Jackie. Jackie cried quietly as he eased her up to seated and wound the cloth around her midsection. Hannah gave what was left of the sheet, which was most of it, to Dogface and pointed at Maddie. He shook out the material and used it to cover the corpse. The centermost side of the shroud quickly wicked blood halfway up the body.

While the men were occupied with taking care of the twins, Hannah found Dogface's bag and rifled through it.

"Hey man, what the fuck?" Dogface started in. But then he saw what she was doing and said, "Oh."

Hannah threw the Lizard Woman a t-shirt and a pair of drawstring shorts, but it was as if the scaled lady didn't know what to do with them. She batted them away and continued to cower. Again, Hannah sighed with her shoulders. She walked toward the frightened creature.

"I'm sorry. I'm so sorry. Please. I didn't mean to hurt anyone," the woman said as she tried to back up farther into the wall behind her.

Hannah held up her hands, palms forward, telling her, "I mean you no harm." The Headless Lady moved slowly toward the Lizard Woman. Reaching out, she touched the scared woman's scaled arm, gently as first, and then taking firm hold of it. At this physical contact, the Lizard Woman went limp, as if finally realizing she was caught and at the mercy of these people, as if she'd lost all hope.

Hannah hugged her.

The Lizard Woman sobbed softly as Hannah dressed her the way she would have dressed a small child, sliding the shirt over her head, lifting her arms through the sleeves one at a time.

While this was happening, Shiva tried to get information from the newcomer.

"Do you have a name?"

"No. I mean, maybe?"

"What do you think it is? Who do you want to be?"

"Wendy?"

"Okay, Wendy, we need to call an ambulance, but the landline is dead. Do you have a cell phone?"

"N-no," she snorted tear-snot back into her head, "but there are other people here who might."

Dogface butted in, addressing Shiva. "It's a fucking dead space for cell phones, hombre. If one don't work for 911, none of them will. Why don't we just take the van?"

Shiva replied to him without looking away from Wendy, "The van would never make it in this storm. You heard it when we pulled in here. But another cell phone might be on a different network or something. We have to try." He asked Wendy, "Do they have one in the front office?"

"Don't go there. Don't go. Don't go to the front office. Don't," Wendy's words tumbled out of her like a rockslide.

"Whoa, okay. Why not?"

"They are bad." She curled back up into a ball and Hannah had to pry her legs out to finish dressing her.

"Okay. You said there are others here?"

"Room 10 and, and, and 7 and 4 have people. They might have phones."

Hannah found some flip-flops among the twins' things. She held them for a moment and cast them to the side. They'd never work with the Lizard Woman's webbed toes. She continued digging in their bags until she found some sandals. After sliding them onto Wendy's feet, Hannah turned toward Dogface and pointed her right hand's first two fingers toward his eyes and then toward Jackie and the Lizard Woman: "Watch them."

Rain beat staccato on the corrugated tin that covered the walkway as the women passed Room 2. Virginia heard a scream die down and looked at Leslie, who raised an eyebrow.

"Who knows what their kind gets up to," Leslie said. "No doubt we'll find out later, when we have to clean up their mess."

"Or you could just have Jasper do the housekeeping tomorrow, especially since he called in because of this storm," Virginia offered.

"Right you are, Ginny. You do have a way of solving problems."

It was music to Virginia's ears. That was all she ever wanted—recognition for making Leslie's life easier. It was her sole motivation in life since the day she'd checked in. She was just passing through, but when she saw how harried Leslie was with three sets of new check-ins, including a gaggle of rambunctious children, and the phone ringing off the hook, Virginia couldn't just stand there and watch. She had to jump in and start helping. And she'd been helping ever since.

When the women got to Room 4, Leslie unlocked the door and went in. Virginia followed her. They were wearing flowered aprons and dish gloves; Virginia hoped it would be enough. It certainly hadn't been last time.

The incredibly large woman on the bed sat up.

"Who are you?" she asked, like it was her motel and not theirs.

Virginia approached the bed while Leslie headed for the bathroom.

"We're here to make sure you're enjoying your stay. Is there anything you need?"

"There's no reason to lie to her," Leslie said, returning from the bathroom and shoving a washcloth in the fat woman's mouth. She looked down at her victim. "We're here to fix you."

Virginia had seen panic before, but there was something different about how this one searched out their eyes—as if she were looking for something inside them that might help her, save her.

"Hold her down, Ginny," Leslie said, snapping Virginia back to the task at hand. Virginia tried and failed to get control of the woman's massive arms.

"She's strong for a fatty," Leslie said, intervening. Together the women folded one arm at a time, so the Fat Lady's squishy hands were near her broad shoulders, and Virginia held them there by the wrists.

Leslie pulled out a carving knife, which she'd brought from their heavily decorated kitchen, and slit the woman's nightgown from neck to hem. Yards of fabric fell away, revealing a giant mound of mottled pink flesh.

"Time to get you down to size," Leslie said with a smile. She lined up the tip of the knife to a spot above and to the right of the navel. Then, she plunged the knife into the rubbery skin and drew it down in a slash the length of a box of butter. The flesh receded from the wound in a bloody line. Leslie slashed again, in the opposite direction, creating an X, and the center of the wound opened up, spilling out yellow fat globules, red tissue, and the brown contents of the woman's digestive tract.

Virginia looked away. But when she heard Leslie say, "Let me see if I can't help this along," she was compelled to turn back.

Leslie put her hands on either side of the Fat Lady's stomach and squeezed. At first the yellow and red and brown liquids continued to seep out.

"Gotta put a little oomph into it, I guess," Leslie said, bearing down on what to her couldn't have been more than a human zit.

And it worked. Something inside gave way and the fat woman's guts came splorching out, with force, all over Leslie. Not just liquids and tapioca-tissue but organs—whole organs and a whole lot of organs—especially what Virginia thought must have been ropes of small intestines, but she was pretty sure she saw a pancreas, too. And there was no mistaking the smack of the liver when it slapped Leslie in the face, ending the deluge of gore.

Headless Hannah and four-armed Shiva raced diagonally across the parking lot. Hannah rapped her knuckles on the door marked 7. A naked man answered. He was gruesomely skinny and had dreadlocks, which he came by naturally, judging from his matted pubic hair. A compact young woman sat on the bed, also naked and not the least ashamed of it. Hannah lifted her hand, the middle three fingers folded in, and held the hang loose sign up to where her head would have been, giving the universal symbol for telephone.

"Uh, sure," the emaciated man said, peeling his eyes away from the Headless Lady. "It's right over there." And he whipped his dreads around, turning his head to look at the phone on the bedside table.

Shiva walked over and picked up the phone. He tried 0. He tried 9.

"Nothing," he said. "Do you have a cell?"

"Yeah, but it's got no charge. Hasn't been charged for weeks. I don't even know if it works anymore," said the naked man.

"Where is it? Is it plugged in?" Shiva asked.

"Uh," the walking skeleton looked around. He went to a pile of what looked like trash on the dresser. There were paper bags and food wrappers and other seemingly random things, like knit hats and glass beads and plastic kazoos. He dug through the heap, letting most of it fall to the floor.

"Here it is!" he said, holding up a shiny black rectangle.

"All right!" Shiva said, taking a few steps toward him.

"Now we just need a charger," said the bony young man.

"Fuck!" Shiva said. He looked back at the door, but Hannah wasn't there. She was already on her way to the only other room occupied by someone who wasn't with the Main Event Sideshow.

Hannah knocked hard on the door of Room 10. It wasn't latched and flew open. The G-man's face registered surprise while his body reacted with smooth movements that came from years of conditioning. He lifted his gun and shot her. She collapsed on the sidewalk.

Shiva covered the last ten feet between himself and Hannah in a heartbeat. He dropped to the walkway next to her and held her in all of his arms.

"Hannah? Hannah, baby, are you hurt?"

She couldn't answer. Her arms lay limp at her sides. Shiva felt warm blood seep across his clothes. He lifted her shirt and saw the bullet hole in her abdomen.

"Oh, baby," he said. "Oh no." He held her tighter.

The G-man put the gun down on the bed. He was stunned for several reasons, not least of which was that he had never, ever missed a kill shot. But then again, everything he'd ever shot had a head. That might explain why he hit her so low on her torso.

He watched as Hannah struggled to lift a hand to Shiva's face. She stroked his cheek and placed her index finger to his lips. He kissed it.

Shiva looked up at the G-man. "You shot her."

"I'm sorry. She startled me. I didn't expect someone with no head. I didn't know." The G-man's face showed his honesty, his confusion and regret.

Dogface appeared next to Shiva, beckoned by the noise of the gunshot.

"He shot her," Shiva said, without looking away from the man in the room. "Hold her."

Shiva laid the love of his life gently on Dogface's lap and stood up, four balls worth of testosterone coursing through his body. He entered the room.

"I didn't mean to," the G-man said, his eyes darting between the hairy new freak and the one stalking toward him. He put his hands up, palms forward. "It was a reflex. I'd never seen a headless person before. I didn't even know there was such a thing."

"She isn't a *thing*," Shiva said through his teeth.

"Sorry. I'm sorry. Fuck, I couldn't be sorrier. I have a first aid kit in my car. I can patch her up and we'll get her to a hospital."

Shiva took the last step, closing the distance between them.

"Don't," Dogface said from the walkway, his voice serious for the first time either of them could remember. "There are more important things to think about right now than revenge. We've got to get Hannah to a hospital. Jackie too."

Without looking away from his prey, Shiva said, "Get Kitten to figure it out. I have to take care of this guy."

"Kitten isn't answering her door," Dogface said.

This piece of information broke Shiva's focus on the G-man. "What do you mean, Kitten isn't answering her door?"

"I knocked hard, man. There isn't a sound coming from inside her room," Dogface said.

They both knew how unlike their boss that was.

"Can you see in her window?" Shiva asked, turning away from the G-man toward the open door as if to see for himself. But he was brought up short by Hannah's sprawled body. His face fell from the tense anger he'd been projecting toward the G-man to absolute sorrow.

"Come on, man. Let's regroup for a minute," Dogface said. "I left Jackie alone with that fucking fish girl, Wendy. We need to get back there before Jackie starts thinking about revenge too."

"Okay," Shiva said, "But this asshole's coming with us. He needs to pay for what he's done." He turned toward Hannah's shooter. "You got a problem with that?" The G-man didn't resist.

The two friends lifted Hannah from the bloodstained pavement.

"Just a sec," Dogface said, shifting the light body into Shiva's arms. He stepped into the shabby motel room and picked up the gun from the bed.

"Fucking guns," he said, smoothly ejecting the magazine and emptying the chamber. "Only fucking douche canoes carry fucking guns." He put the bullets in the pocket of his shorts and the gun in his waistband. "Right. Let's go."

CHAPTER 5
NO WAY OUT

"Should we check it out? Think they need help?" The stocky young woman stood at the window trying to see up the walkway and make out figures through the rain. Every muscle in her body was wound up, ready to spring into action. Her straight black bangs poked in her eyes—the kind of eyes that led a certain type of person to ask her where she's from.

"We shouldn't get involved. We're laying low, remember?" Rail said from the bed.

Ox sighed. There was something about the way he said "laying low" that made it sound like he was excited about it— like they were some bigtime outlaws on the run, instead of two dirty kids who ripped off the last people who did right by them.

"Are the clothes dry?" she asked, still considering going out there, seeing if someone was hurt. Maybe they could use her. She could be really useful to have around.

Rail rolled off the bed and went into the bathroom, where they had hung their clothes after washing them in the tub. Ox didn't envy the cleaning lady who would have to deal with that scum ring.

"They're still kinda moist. Probably because of the rain," he said as he flumped back onto the bed.

That settled that. She couldn't go out there naked.

"C'mon, Ox. It's for the best. Wanna see what's on TV?"

Ox huffed. TV was the furthest thing from her mind. She couldn't believe he would suggest something so banal knowing someone might be in serious trouble just a few doors down. This was probably one of those red flags people said to watch out for. She'd only just met Rail three months earlier at the gathering in Tennessee. It was definitely not too late to bail. But she liked him, and he was the best travel buddy ever. People couldn't help but want to feed him. She'd eaten better every day of the last three months than any day of her last two years on the road.

It wasn't that he didn't eat. He did. And he was always hungry, too. He said it was some kind of autoimmune disorder. He'd spent his whole life in the hospital with tubes and wires going in and coming out all over. Then, the minute he turned eighteen, he unplugged himself and jumped a train, no idea where it was headed. He broke his wrist doing it too, because he tried to jump a freight on a straightaway.

That kind of life, of sickness and immobility, was hard for Ox to imagine, which was probably why she was with him— she felt bad for him, wanted to take care of him. And she could, in her way.

While he'd been sick in bed, she'd been out playing hard and working hard, helping her parents on their hardscrabble organic permaculture ultra-elite frou-frou ranch. Call it what you will, it was still ranching. So it wasn't long before they noticed she was one hardy little girl, to put it mildly. For as long as Ox could remember, she didn't get sick, she could lift twice her weight, and she didn't feel pain. She could get hurt; she just didn't feel it when it happened. This wasn't always a blessing. There were plenty of times she'd come home with tree-branch-sized slivers through her flesh or rusty nails spiked through her feet. But that didn't change the fact that her whole childhood, she lived to be outside, throwing artisanal hay bales and bringing in bushels of hand-picked heirloom gooseberries.

But right around the time she finished school, the ranch had gone under and her parents divorced. She tried the whole apartment-and-a-job-in-the-city thing. She lasted one month. Since then she'd been riding the rails and hitching her way across the country, happy just to be outside.

For now, though, she was stuck inside.

"Fine," she said. "Give me the remote."

He couldn't. It was bolted to the nightstand.

The three men sloshed their way across the parking lot, hunched and squinting against the driving rain, lit by lightning and rattled by thunder every few seconds. Dogface and the G-man walked in front, while Shiva carried Hannah behind them, the way a groom carries a bride over a threshold. When they came to the door of Room 2, Dogface used his key to open it.

Jackie had moved from Maddie's deathbed to the bed by the window. She had also changed out of her blood-soaked clothes and into camo-colored cargo shorts and a black tank top, the kind of shirt Maddie liked because it draped over their connection. Her bag sat open on the bed, and Wendy was handing her pills out of a small white bottle of ibuprofen. The Lizard Woman held a flimsy plastic cup to the lips of the no-longer-conjoined twin until Jackie lifted her hand to say, "No more."

"Thank God for cramps, huh?" Jackie said with a sardonic smile as Dogface walked in. Then, seeing the rest of them spill into the room, making dark spots on the carpet with their wet shoes and the water dripping off them, she asked, "What's wrong with Hannah?"

"Ask this asshole," Shiva said, gesturing with his chin toward the G-man. He laid Hannah on the bed next to Jackie.

"Well?" Jackie asked, taking in Hannah's bloody shirt and ragged breathing. Her voice grew fierce, "What's the story, asshole?"

"My name is Bill," he said. "What's yours?"

"Oh no, you don't get to play that card right now," Jackie said. "We've all seen the PSA: to humanize yourself to your attacker, your mugger, your rapist, tell them your name. Us freaks use that shit all the time. But you don't get to." She stopped to take a breath and winced, hitching her hand to her injured side. "So, I guess I'll just go ahead and assume you did something dumb and now Hannah is really hurt."

"I shot her," Bill said.

"How bad is it?" she asked, looking back at Hannah's struggling body next to her. "Is she going to make it?"

"She's alive," Shiva said. "But just barely. We have to get an ambulance here, now."

"Okay, so, does this asshole have a cell phone?"

Shiva looked at Bill, who shook his head.

"Bullshit, motherfucker," Dogface said. "Look at this chump. He has to have a cell phone."

"I broke it," Bill said.

"Oh wait, shit." Shiva started looking around.

"What? Did you try the office?" Jackie asked.

"No," Shiva said. "The kids in Room 7 have a phone. I just need to get them a charger. If that doesn't work, I'll have to try the office."

"Don't!" Wendy said from where she stood by the bed, still holding Jackie's water cup.

"Jesus Christ, woman, why the fuck not?" asked Dogface.

"They don't like people like us, people who are different. I mean, they *really don't like freaks.* They're evil."

"They can't be that bad," Shiva said. "They rented us rooms, didn't they?"

"What did you look like when they saw you?"

Shiva knew immediately what she meant. He'd had his smaller arms shoved in his jacket sleeves.

"All right. I'll grab my jacket from next door in case the kids' phone doesn't work."

Shiva opened the door of the room he shared with Hannah. It still smelled like their sex. The sheets on the bed were thrown back from when they'd heard Jackie's screams and gone running to help.

Shiva picked up the phone charger, smudged his tears across his cheeks, and put on his jacket. Then he headed back out into the rain.

He ran over to Room 7 and knocked. The young woman answered. He held the cord out in front of him.

"Can we try this? Please, it's important."

She wasted no time plugging in the phone. The three of them, with one set of clothes between them, stared at the dark screen, waiting, with the television babbling in the background.

"What's going on?" the girl asked Shiva without looking away from the phone.

As they waited, Shiva told them what happened. He felt as if he were watching himself from some back corner of his mind as he recited the events of that night—from Wendy falling through the ceiling, ripping the twins apart and killing Maddie; to holding Jackie's body down while Hannah burned the wound closed; to Hannah getting shot; to still not knowing why Kitten wasn't answering her door. Ox and Rail listened, dumbfounded.

Finally the phone did something. The screen flashed a blinding white and went dark again just as fast. The red symbol of an empty battery glowed for a second. Then nothing.

Shiva pressed the power button. The battery symbol lit up and faded. He did it again and the same thing happened.

"Shit. How long will this take?" he asked.

"I don't know, man. I'm sorry," Rail answered.

"Fuck it. It was a long shot anyway. It probably won't even work if it's charged. I just can't sit around doing nothing. I'm going to try the office. But if they don't have a means of calling out, is it okay if I come back here and check on this thing later?"

"Of course," Ox said. "And let us know if there's anything else we can do to help."

"Thanks," Shiva said, not sure why he'd need the help of a little girl and a guy whose hip sockets were clearly visible through his skin, but if Shiva knew anything, it was that you never knew. "I appreciate it," he said.

The chimes on the door handle stopped tinkling, but no one came out from the back. Shiva rang the desk bell three times, fast, but still no one showed. He reached over the desk and picked up the phone. No dial tone.

"Hello?" The voice came from the back. "Hold on. I'll be right with you." And a minute later the kindly-looking, sarcastic woman he'd met before came out. She was buttoning the wrist cuffs of her flannel shirt. The skin on her face and hands was bright red, as if freshly scrubbed, and she seemed out of breath.

"Hi there," she said with a great big smile. "What can I do ya for?"

"There's been an accident. Two accidents. My girlfriend's been shot and my friend is hurt. I need to call 911 but all the phones are out."

"Are they?" she asked. "That's weird. Here, let me try." She picked up the phone and punched the three numbers. She covered the receiver and said, "It's ringing." Then, uncovering it, she said, "Hello? Yes, this is Virginia over at the Sleep E-Z Motel. There's been an accident. We need an ambulance right away." She looked off into the middle distance like she was listening, and then mouthed at Shiva, "And cops?" He nodded.

"Yes, send the police too. Quickly!" She paused again and then said, "Yes . . . No . . . That's right. Okay. Thank you. Thank you so much." She hung up.

"They'll be here just as quick as they can. Is there anything I can do for you while we wait? A first aid kit? More towels?"

"No," Shiva said, moving toward the door. "No, we're okay for now. Thank you for making the call. I need to get back." And he was gone.

"Wendy was right," Shiva said after rushing back to the room. "There's something really wrong with the woman running this place. She just pretended to have a complete conversation with a 911 operator in front of me."

"Was her hair red or brownish-gray?" the Lizard Woman asked.

"Brownish. Why?"

"Because she's not even the crazy one! We need to get out of here. We can hide in the well."

"Do what now?" Dogface asked. "That seems a little drastic to me. Anybody want to back me up on this?"

"It's a long story," Wendy said, "but the short version is they will kill you. You have to hide."

"Yeah right," Dogface said.

"No, really. I've seen it happen."

Dogface considered the Lizard Woman. He might have been a goofball, a party kid, and a loudmouth, but he knew enough about people to know when they were scared shitless and when it was time to get serious.

"Alright then," Dogface said. "But we don't need to hide in your skanky ass well. We'll just take our chances with the van. Who's got the keys?"

"Right here," Shiva said from where he stood next to Hannah's side of the bed. He pulled the keys out of the front pocket of his pants.

"It's not skanky," Wendy said.

Everyone stopped and looked at her.

"My well. It isn't skanky. It's actually kind of nice."

"Still, we should leave while we motherfucking can," Dogface said. He looked around, considering their situation and formulating a plan. "Shiva, you and Wendy help Jackie and Hannah to the van and Cunt Shart," he pointed a furry finger at Bill, "and I will get Kitten."

Shiva nodded and Dogface clapped his hands like they were breaking from a huddle. He and Bill left the room, heading for Kitten, and Shiva turned his attention to Jackie.

"Can you walk?" he asked.

"'Course I can," she said, forcing a smile. She swung her legs over the side of the bed and used her arms to press herself up to sitting. Her eyes went blank.

"She's lost a lot of blood," Wendy said.

"Hey there, Jackie? Still with us?" Shiva asked.

"Yeah, just give me a second. And maybe some of that water." Wendy helped her take a few sips.

"Here we go," she said, hoisting herself to her feet only to list and then fall to her left. She was so used to her sister counterbalancing her, she didn't know how to stand on her own.

"Whoa there," Shiva said. "It's okay. We've got you." He and Wendy supported her from either side.

To Wendy he said, "Let's get her out to the van and make sure it's going to run before we try to move Hannah." And then to the love of his life he said, "We'll be right back for you, baby. I love you."

Shiva and Wendy supported Jackie between them as they went out into the rain.

When they got to the van, they opened the side door. Wendy slid across the bench seat and helped Shiva maneuver Jackie beside her. Then Shiva squeezed through to the driver's seat. He turned the key and the van coughed, turning over but not catching, not starting. He tried the key again. Same thing.

"Shit," Shiva said. "Shit. Shit. Shit."

Dogface knocked on Kitten's door.

"Why does she need help getting to the van?" Bill asked.

"She's over six hundred pounds, fuckwad," Dogface replied. "She can hardly stand up without help."

Bill said nothing. Dogface knocked again. "Kitten? We gotta go. Can we come in?"

Still nothing. Dogface tried the knob. It was locked. He cupped his hands around his eyes, trying to see in the window, but there were no lights on inside.

"Want me to break the door down?" Bill asked.

"What are you, Mr. Buzzcut? Are you a cop? You're totally a cop. Oh! Oh! Can I call you Cunt-stubble Bill?"

"Knock yourself out. You want me to break us into this room or not?"

"Or we could not break anything and just go in through this open window," Dogface said.

"That'll work."

Reaching over the air conditioner, Dogface popped off the screen and worked his fingers into the crack where the sideways sliding window was not quite closed. Metal rubbed metal as he worked it open. Then he hoisted himself up and over, landing in the small space between the bed and the wall. He moved out of the way, and Cunt-stubble Bill did the same.

"Holy fucknuts. It smells worse than old lady queefs in here. What the fuck, Kitten?"

Dogface flipped the switch for the overhead light.

Kitten's bed was a fatty, bloody, shitty mess. It looked as if her insides had been squeezed out through a pie-sized hole in her stomach.

Bill puked on the carpet.

"Nice one, Super Cop," Dogface said to Bill. Turning back toward Kitten, he exhaled an "Oh Jesus" as he got closer to her, trying to make sense of what he was seeing.

Kitten reached out for him. He peed a little.

"Save the girl in the well," she said, and then she breathed her last.

Virginia waved Leslie around the corner.

"Stupid freaks. Think I don't know what's going on in my own motel," Leslie muttered as Virginia opened the door to Room 2. Leslie couldn't. Her hands were full.

The women stood just inside the door. There was blood everywhere inside the little room: dark splotches and drips on the floor; a bright red swath in the far corner; on the farther bed, a body-shaped island of white rose up out of a burgundy lake; and the near bed held Headless Hannah, whose own blood covered her clothes and arms and was turning dark brown as it dried.

"Jesus Christ," Leslie said. "What a shit show."

"My word, would you look at that!" Virginia said. "No head! How do you think she manages?" She was right up on the young woman now. "These must be how she eats and breathes," she said, inspecting the top of Hannah's neck stump and pointing to the skin flaps that fluttered once every few seconds. "This girl's near dead already, Leslie. I don't think there's any more work to be done here."

"Don't be ridiculous, Ginny. We can't let her die a freak. She needs to be whole. She needs to be a real girl before she passes on."

Virginia didn't answer. She just watched as Leslie unscrewed the head of the broom she'd brought with her.

"Hold this," Leslie said, handing her the broomstick. "Angle it toward me."

Virginia held the rod tight as Leslie slammed a honeydew down onto it, piercing the melon through the bottom but not the top. Then Leslie brought out a Sharpie and drew three lines on it: two for eyes and one for an overly wide smile.

"There," Leslie said. "That'll do nicely."

She took the pole from Virginia and set it against the wall. "Help me set her up," she said.

The women worked together to maneuver Hannah's barely breathing body so her back was against the pressed-wood headboard.

Leslie climbed on the bed, wobbling and catching her balance before reaching out her hand to Virginia for the broomstick. She lined up the non-meloned end of it with one of Hannah's throat holes, then lifted it up about a foot and slammed it down.

It didn't slide in as easily as she'd thought it would. She had to work hard at it, maneuvering the stick around when it caught on the girl's ribs or spine or pelvis. Sometime during her efforts, the body stopped struggling. That made it easier. Finally, she hit bottom, but two feet of broomstick still stuck out of the Headless Lady's neck.

"Oh well," Leslie said. "Can't let the perfect be the enemy of the good." And she placed her hands on either side of the melon-head and slid it down the pole to nest on Hannah's neck.

Jackie waited. She waited for the painkillers to kick in, even a little bit. She waited while Shiva got out of the van, back into the pelting rain, and popped the hood. She waited for the shock and numbness to wear off and the reality of her missing sister to sink in.

Shiva dropped the hood and got back in the van.

"They cut the wire to the distributor. We're not going anywhere."

"What do we do now?" Jackie asked.

"I'm telling you, we can hide in the well. It's big. There's a cave down there," Wendy pleaded.

"What about that Bill guy? He has to have a car," Jackie said.

There was one other car in the parking lot, a white Chevy Malibu.

"You're right," Shiva said. "Stay here." And he was back out in the rain.

But Jackie wasn't having it. "Fuck that," she said to Wendy. "I'm not waiting here. Help me with this door."

Wendy helped Jackie out of the van. They ducked under the cover of the walkway and nearly ran into Shiva, who was standing outside Room 4, Kitten's room. Just then, the door opened and Dogface and Bill stepped out.

"Oh good Lord," Jackie said, leaning heavily on Wendy. "What is that stench?"

"It's Kitten," Dogface said. "She's dead. Her insides are on her outsides."

"What?" Shiva and Jackie said together.

"Yeah, man. I wouldn't even fucking look if I were you. I wish I could unsee it, that's for damn fucking sure."

For a moment, no one moved, no one spoke. They just stood in the cloud of Kitten's death smell, overwhelmed by her murder and realizing the danger they were in.

The pause was broken by Jackie.

"Can you get me her canes?" she asked Dogface.

"What?"

"Her canes," she said, flashing her eyes toward Wendy, the woman who killed her sister, on whom she was relying to stand. "To help me walk. Please?"

Dogface took a deep breath and went back into the room.

"You can take my car, if you want," Bill said.

Shiva nodded and Dogface came gasping back out of the room.

"Here," he said, handing the canes to Jackie. "They were by the head of the bed, so out of the splash zone."

"We're taking Bill's car," Shiva said to Dogface. "Let's go."

They stayed near the building to avoid the rain as much as they could. After the first few steps, which she spent bobbling and slipping, Jackie figured out how to walk under her own volition, though Wendy hovered nearby, just in case.

When they were in front of Room 10, Bill's room, Bill started to hand Shiva the keys to his car but then stopped and turned toward Dogface.

"Can I have my gun back?"

"No, motherfucker, you may not have your motherfucking gun back."

"Look, you can take my car, just give me back my gun. I'm not going to shoot anybody else after tonight."

Shiva interrupted, "No way. You're coming with us. We'll figure out what to do with you later. But no way are you going free."

"I came here to kill myself, and I'm not leaving until I do."

The four freaks looked at each other. Again, everyone was quiet for a minute.

"But if you do kill yourself," Jackie said, "you wouldn't be leaving here at all."

"Maybe," Dogface said, puzzling it out as he spoke, "he means like his soul would be free to leave?"

Wendy chimed in, "I think he just means to say he wants to kill himself and he doesn't want to go somewhere else to do it."

Bill, exasperated, said, "You know what I mean. Give me my gun and you won't have to worry about me anymore."

"Yeah," said Dogface. "No fucking way, Cunt-stubble Bill. Get in the car." And he swiped the keys from the man's hand.

"God! Finally!" Jackie said, leaning heavily on Kitten's canes.

Jackie had been standing closest to the edge of the walkway, and therefore was the closest to the Chevy. So she was the first one to turn around and see that they wouldn't be taking that car either.

"Got two spares?" she asked, speaking loudly over the storm.

Shiva and Dogface moved beside her.

"Fuck," they said in unison.

"Now can we go to the well?" Wendy asked.

The group agreed they were out of other options.

"We'll need the ladder from around back," Wendy said. "To get the injured down there."

"You guys get that," Shiva said. "Dogface, come help me with Hannah."

"Oh, hold on." Wendy grabbed the welcome mats from in front of Rooms 9 and 10. "Okay, let's go."

CHAPTER 6
DOWN THE WELL

Wendy draped the welcome mats over the rim of the well, over the worn-down shards of multi-colored glass. "You'll still want to be careful, but these should help," she said to the people behind her.

At the base of the ladder, Wendy lit a flashlight and perched it on a rock to keep it out of the pooling water. Then she found her way through a hole in the sidewall of the well. The hole led to a slope, a wet slide, that dropped another ten feet or so downward. At the bottom of that, Wendy set about lighting a mixed bag of lanterns and candles and more flashlights until the cave glowed amber.

Jackie was the first of the others to enter the Lizard Woman's home. She was followed quickly by Bill and then Dogface.

"Where's Shiva?" Jackie asked.

"Hannah is dead. He'll be here when he gets here," Dogface said.

"Fuck," Jackie said. She tore into Bill with her glare. "You killed her!"

"No," Dogface told her. "It was worse than that. It was *them*, whoever did Kitten did Hannah, too."

Shiva showed up at the cave entrance, his face wet from the rain, but his eyes more red than just the weather could make them. He shuffled down the ramp, shoulders low, head hung—his whole body expressing his sorrow.

The newcomers stood together, the four of them, taking in their refuge.

The cave was at least as big as two of the motel rooms put together, but its ceiling wasn't quite as high. There were a few stalagmites and stalactites and a couple of rocky outcroppings, but on the whole the floor was smooth. To the left were cases of water and soda and stacks of food, the kinds of things you would take with you traveling, plenty of trail mix and beef jerky. And on the other side of the cave was a small hill of pillows, colorful in their white, pink, blue, and cartooned pillowcases. There was also a smaller pile of blankets and sleeping bags.

A stream trickled through the middle of the earthen room. It left by way of a dark tunnel on the far side that was much taller and wider than the little stream needed, large enough for a person to walk through if they stooped, or if they weren't very tall to begin with.

"Please, make yourselves at home," Wendy said. It was a line she'd often heard but never thought she'd use.

The men grabbed drinks and sat down. It was their first breather since Wendy had fallen through the ceiling. They were all out of adrenaline, and each of them sank into themselves. Shiva sat on a boulder, hiding his eyes behind his bigger hands while his smaller hands cradled his chin. Dogface leaned back against the wet cave wall. Bill sat bolt upright, shoulders back, gaze forward, but Bill looked like the kind of man who could stand comfortably at parade rest for hours. Maybe even sleep there.

Jackie set Kitten's canes aside and eased herself onto a rolled-out sleeping bag. She lay down on her side, the one that hadn't recently been ripped open and burned closed. Wendy rushed to get her a bottle of water and a little sleeve of mixed nuts.

"Is there anything else you need?" Wendy asked.

Jackie waved her away.

Quiet settled over them and Jackie's mind turned to her sister. Jackie had been beside herself with joy to finally find a home among the freaks, but she would have given it all up in one shared heartbeat to have her sister back again. She knew Maddie only agreed to join the troupe to make her happy. Guilt blossomed in her chest and sent strong roots into her belly. By the time Shiva's voice echoed off the cave walls, she had carefully catalogued her every failing as a sister.

"Must help a lot," Shiva said, wiping the tears from his face and pointing at the stream. He was talking to Wendy. "With your ichthyosis, must help to live in a damp cave like this."

"What do you mean?" Wendy asked.

"Your ichthyosis, your skin condition."

"Skin condition," Wendy said more to herself than back at him.

"Sure," he said. "It isn't common, but it's not unheard of."

Wendy looked at her arms and legs. She scratched her forearm and hexagons of skin floated down to the cave floor like leaves. "I've never seen anyone else like me," she said. "Not even on TV."

"It's rare, but it happens. It's even made some people famous, like Susi the Elephant Skin Woman and Alice the Alligator Girl." He gestured at the stream again. "Keeping the skin moist keeps the scales from drying up and cracking."

"I bleed a lot just before the rains come," she said.

Shiva was about to respond when something chittered from deep within the cave system. Something was calling out, something angry or worried, or both.

Wendy and the three men all jumped to their feet, but she was the only one who ran toward the sound.

The chittering grew louder after Wendy disappeared into the darkness of the tunnel. It sounded like a mother chipmunk berating her child: high pitched, squeaky, emphatic.

A minute later, Wendy returned and said, "Please don't freak out."

From behind Wendy crept a six-foot-tall albino creature. At first it could have been mistaken for a white wolf walking on its hind legs. But as it got closer, they could see its lower body was almost kangaroo-like, with powerful legs and large, clawed feet. Its upper body was that of an enormous bat, with its arms and wings folded in. A mouth full of fangs spread across its face, and its red irises peered at them. It was covered in fine white hair and had a full-body mohawk of quills from the top of its head down its back.

Wendy held her hands out in front of her, palms forward, webbing spread. "It's just my mom."

"Chupacabra," Bill said under his breath. "Of course it is."

The monster stood close to Wendy, looking from one to the other of their guests.

"See," Wendy said to it. "I told you they weren't dangerous."

The group, exhausted and confounded, stayed completely still. Only their eyes looked to one another, asking unspoken questions: What should we do? Should we run? Should we act like this is normal?

No one moved until Jackie, who had been leaning on her hands, caught in the middle of sitting up, started to push herself to seated and Wendy ran to help her. As if to follow her, the albino chupacabra stepped forward, moving farther into the light of the cave.

Dogface was the first to speak, though he did so out of the side of his mouth.

"We should be getting the fuck out of here, shouldn't we?" He slid his eyes to the side to look at Shiva. "I mean, this is pretty fucked up right here, isn't it?"

Nobody answered him. Neither Shiva nor Bill even twitched in his direction.

"What I'm trying to say," Dogface said, working hard to keep his voice calm, "is that I do not feel very fucking safe right now and would like very fucking much to get the fuck out of here."

"No!" Wendy said. "You can't go up there. They'll kill you. You saw what they did to your friends."

"Yeah, well," Dogface said, "I saw what you did to my friend too. And I saw what he did to my friend too." He tilted his head ever so slightly toward Bill. "Maybe it was something like that? Maybe they didn't mean it either."

"You can't believe that," Wendy said. "Look, I am sorry—no, sorry isn't strong enough. I am devastated. I am not sure how, or if, I'm going to be able to live with myself after tonight. But what they did to your Fat Lady, whatever happened to Hannah, those weren't accidents.

"Listen," she began, and she told them the story of the night she'd been trying to forget since it happened.

A teenaged Wendy had just watched an episode of *Lost* with the small family in Room 8. Of course, they didn't know she was in the ceiling, but it gave Wendy a sense of comfort to be close to the mother and father and their little one. The infant, too small to walk but big enough to crawl around and make mischief, had fallen asleep just after the first commercial break.

The Lizard Girl hadn't understood a lot of what happened in the episode, and based on the conversation between the mother and father, they hadn't either. She believed, as they did, that if she just kept watching, soon everything would be explained.

The parents turned off the TV and were going to bed, and the only other room with people, Room 6, held a trio, two women and one man, who were tying each other up and doing naked things. Wendy wasn't interested.

She knew she should wait. It wasn't late enough, but she was antsy. She made her way down from the crawlspace.

Because of TV, Wendy recognized the two cars in the lot as a Camry and an Odyssey—two of the "best selling cars of the year," which she assumed meant a lot of them were on the road. Still, it was odd to have such new models at their motel. Usually the cars she had to work with were older, sometimes really old. But older cars were good for Wendy. She could use the wire hanger trick, another thing she learned from TV. With new cars she could only hope they had been left unlocked. They rarely were, but she always tried.

The minivan side door slid open. A chorus of angels sang and the mound of treasure directly in front of her emitted a golden glow. There were gallons of water; bags of goldfish crackers and little tubs of fruit (fruit!); and a soft, fuzzy blanket. Chunks of skin rained down inside the van as she loaded her arms with as much as she could carry.

Three steps toward the well, she heard a room door open behind her. She quickened her pace.

"Hey!" the mother's voice called out. "Hey! What are you doing? Get back here with that!"

Wendy reached the edge of the glass field and had to slow down. The mother was going to catch up to her. The mother had shoes and could walk on the glass. The Lizard Girl turned around, ready to forfeit her treasure. Ready to face whatever consequences were coming.

"What on earth?" the mother said, coming to meet her where she stood. "Child, why are you naked? Where are your parents?"

Before the bewildered teen could answer, there was an ear-splitting bang. Startled, she dropped her precious find. Fruit cups hit the pavement, popped open, oozed their gooey syrup and spongy chunks. The mother fell to the ground. Her eyes were open. Blood spilled out the side of her head, creating a black puddle on the gray asphalt.

This wasn't what death looked like on TV. On TV, their faces looked soft. On TV, it didn't mess up their hair. On TV, you couldn't feel the absence, the difference between when they were here and when, one second later, they were gone. On TV, they didn't look so very dead.

"Virginia!" The voice registered in a hollow deep within the girl's mind, but she didn't dare move. "Bring the pistol."

Wendy wrenched her eyes away from the woman on the ground and toward the woman with the rusty red hair, toward Leslie, just in time to watch her fire her shotgun again. She followed the aim of the barrel and saw the man, the father, duck behind the minivan.

The other woman, Virginia, came out with a handgun. She said something to Leslie that Wendy couldn't hear.

Leslie exchanged guns with Virginia and then shooed her back toward the office. She stalked across the parking lot. When she turned the corner around the van, the man, who was crumpled up like an empty bag of chips, said, "No. Please. I have a daughter in there."

Leslie shot the man point blank.

The people in Room 6 were at their window, fingers making spaces in the blinds. Leslie and the Lizard Girl saw them at the same time.

Fishing her keyring from her elbow, where it lived on a curly spring of orange plastic, Leslie walked to Room 6. She calmly tucked the pistol in the waistband of her jeans and tried the doorknob. It was locked. She used the key, opened the door, and disappeared inside the room.

Wendy, still rooted to the spot, heard screaming, then gunshots.

During the shooting, one of the women ran naked from the room, tripping over her own feet. She tried the car doors. When they didn't open, she ran up the walkway, away from Leslie, who had just come out of the room alone. The woman tried the door to Room 7. It didn't open. She kept running, hunched in on herself, as if trying to protect her vulnerable, soft front side, as if her back side wasn't just as vulnerable. When she got to Room 8, where the family had been, she tried the door. It opened.

The baby's crying, which Wendy noticed now for the first time, grew louder and quieter again with the opening and closing of the door.

When Leslie got to Room 8, she didn't have her gun anymore. She tucked her hair behind her ears, smoothed down her shirt, and reached for the knob. It turned but the door didn't open. Leslie pressed her shoulder against the door and pushed, budging it one slow inch at a time, until she could slip inside.

There were more screams. Broken glass. And then there was nothing. No sound, no light. When Leslie came out of Room 8, there was no baby crying.

Virginia came back out of the office and headed for Leslie. "What is going on?" she asked.

When Leslie turned toward Virginia, Wendy tried to take advantage of the distraction. She stepped onto the glass, trying to be as quiet as she could be. Trying to be invisible.

"You! Freak!" It was Leslie's voice, like a nest of scorpions scuttling over each other. "This is your fault."

The teenager hurried. The skin on her feet was tough, but still the glass bit in.

As she hopped over the jagged ring of shards circling the top of the well, Wendy heard Virginia say, "Leslie, what is that?"

The Lizard Girl lowered herself down fast, missing familiar finger and toe holds, scraping her knees and forearms.

The women appeared above her, just their heads and shoulders framed by the circle of stones.

"What was that?" Virginia asked again.

"It's a goddamn freak is what it is. I shouldn't have let you live. You hear me?" She was yelling down the well now. "I should have killed you the moment I gave birth to you. You're just lucky I haven't ever caught you out of that well."

"That's your child?" Virginia asked. "You can't mean to say you'd kill your own child."

Wendy listened hard. This monster was her mother?

"Doesn't mean a thing that she come out of me—that ain't no human child," Leslie said, still talking down the well. "You saw it. It's a freak of nature, got no place in the natural order. Worse than coloreds and spics. Worse than retards. It's an abomination and killing it wouldn't be no different than swatting a spider."

"Stop it," Virginia said. "You don't mean that."

But the girl in the well knew Leslie meant it. She had watched Leslie—her birth mother—kill those people, people who died only because she had let herself be seen. And those were regular folks.

"See," the full-grown Wendy said to the other freaks in her well, "you can't go up there. I can't let you. I can't be responsible for any more deaths."

CHAPTER 7
WENDY'S MOM

The whole time Wendy had been telling her story, everyone else in the cave—Jackie, Shiva, Dogface, and Bill—had their eyes glued to the chupacabra, who was shuffling her large feet and worrying her paws together, clacking her claws.

"Well, we can't stay here forever," Jackie said. "Sooner or later they're going to figure out we're down here. We've got a gun, and we can get Hannah's machetes and Maddie's throwing knives from the trailer. I say we get these psychos before they can get us."

"You shouldn't be going anywhere," Shiva said. "Least of all into a fight. There's still the possibility of the kids' phone. It's a long shot, but we have to try. It has to have some kind of charge by now."

"We should all go then," Jackie said, side-eyeing the nervous albino creature.

"No, you need to stay here. I'm sorry, Jackie, but you'd just slow me down."

"Seriously?" But she knew he had a point. "Fine. But still, you shouldn't go alone."

"There's a good-sized first aid kit in the trunk of my car. I'll come," Bill said.

Shiva's lips screwed over to one side of his face.

"Or not," Bill said.

Dogface volunteered. "I'll go." He reached into his pocket. "We've already got the keys to the bacon mobile." He tossed them to Shiva.

"Great," Jackie said. "So, I'll just chill down here in this cave with the guy who shot Hannah, the woman who killed my sister, and a chupa-fucking-cabra. Sounds good to me. What could go wrong?"

Wendy and Bill both looked down, away from the conversation they'd been watching.

"You'll be okay," Shiva said. "Bill here is going to make sure of it. Right, Bill?"

"Of course," Bill said, snapping into an even more on-duty posture than before.

Shiva switched to his everything's-going-to-be-alright voice. "Look, you just need to be patient, Jackie, just for a little while longer."

"That's exactly what Maddie would have said." Jackie smiled a sad half grin.

Shiva and Dogface made their way up the slick incline, bracing their hands and feet along the dry outer edges. They crawled through the hole into the well and were gone.

Wendy brought some pillows over to Jackie.

"Stop it, okay. Just stop."

"But I thought you might be more comfortable—"

"I know. I know what you thought. You thought you could ease your guilt about killing my sister by sucking up to me. But guess what—it's not my job to make you feel better. It's my job to be pissed that my twin sister, the girl I've shared every breath with since the day we were born, is dead. The person who knew me so well she could predict what I was going to do when even I didn't know what I was going to do is dead, and it's my job to figure out how to live with having been born with our heart. And having you in my face is not making any of this any fucking easier. So why don't you please just take your pillows and fuck off back to your weird ass mom, make sure she doesn't kill us, and let me manage for myself."

Tears streaked down Wendy's dry face as she walked away from Jackie and sat down next to her mom.

Wendy's mom was worried. All she ever wanted was to be a mother, and if she could be anywhere near as good a mother as her own, then that was all the better. But now there were people in her cave who shouldn't be there, and she didn't know what to do. She wanted to trust her daughter, but she wanted to keep her safe even more. Things had been good for a long time now, but this was bad. Anxiety was bringing up memories she'd rather forget.

Her pack had treated her like she didn't exist, all of them except for her mother.

That there was a pack was a problem. There were too many of them. They'd become conspicuous. The nights that had been quiet, with plentiful sleeping prey, grew chaotic, with blazing lights and loud booms. And while the strong hind legs of their species allowed most of them to escape, a few had been injured and limped away, as their instincts insisted, as far away as they could get before death overtook them.

The pack migrated, moving toward the brightest star, trying to find a new home. But after just one night in new fields, the next night wouldn't be safe. They would move north again. They did this until the herds of goats and sheep and cattle were gone—even the grass was gone—and hunting as a pack didn't work anymore. They had to disperse, to scavenge alone for jackrabbits and rats. If one of them came across enough to share—a family of javelina, a herd of deer—they would call out, chitter their ultrasonic come-and-get-it message to the others: "Blood."

Like so many of them on the long trek, her mother grew weak, and one night after the hunt, her mother didn't come back.

She continued to travel with the others, even though they shunned her. She was different. She was a hazard. She was all white while they were dark green and gray and black—colors that camouflaged them.

When they came across bigger prey, no one would make space for her at the kill the way her mother had. When they loped along all night and she was tired from hunger, they didn't slow down for her.

Another new territory, again the pack split up to search for food. She ranged through scrubby desert bushes, finding nothing for hours. But she persisted. She wandered far, into the foothills of low mountains where there might at least be water.

The instant the sun broke over the horizon, her red eyes squinted defensively, her pale skin flashed with warning pain. She needed to find shelter. As a pack, they slept in abandoned outbuildings, disused barns or cattle sheds, or, when nothing else could be found, they burrowed into the earth. When her mother was alive and they had to hide in the dirt, her mother would lie on top of her to keep her white flesh from burning through the long hours of searing sunlight.

She didn't have time to find the pack.

She scratched at the dirt with her strong claws. Burrowing would be impossible. The ground was too hard.

Peering through her squinting eyes, she scanned the mountain range, clearly visible for miles with no trees to obstruct her view. There—a dark spot. She took flight and sped toward it, expecting an overhang or small dugout created by the torrents of the brief desert rainy season. Instead she found a cave. Not just a cave, but a tunnel. She followed it into the earth.

The next night she stayed in the cave. There was water. There were rats and bats to feed on. There was protection from the sun and from the humans with their noise and violence. None of her pack came looking for her.

One day, years after she'd made a new life for herself in the underground maze, she heard crying. She found the little girl screeching up a cylinder that led to the surface. She heard the voice of an angry human above ground, coming closer. Wrapping the little one in her wing, she ducked out of the light, back into the cave. And from that moment, she was a mother.

"So, Wendy," Bill asked, putting on an air of conversation that made both Wendy and Jackie immediately suspicious.

"Yes?" she answered hesitantly. She had crouched down beside the chupacabra and was petting its back, soothing it.

"Tell me about your mom there. Has she been living with you down here for very long?"

"For as long as I can remember. I mean, I don't remember much of anything from before being down here. Just flashes of some nice old people and a little stuffed lamb for some reason."

"So you've been living down here since you were really young then?"

"Yes," Wendy said, flicking something black and tarry off her fingers.

"With her?"

"Sure, she's always been here. When I was little, she would hold me when I cried. She must have found food for me before I was big enough to do it for myself. I remember her teaching me how."

"And does she eat what you eat?" Bill asked, switching subtly into police questioning mode.

Jackie watched the conversation like a tennis match, waiting for Wendy to realize she was being interrogated. But Wendy either didn't notice or didn't care.

"Oh no. She can only drink blood. Over the summer she feeds on bats that nest farther down in the caves, but in the winter they leave and she has to go out and hunt."

"Does she ever hunt humans, that you know of?"

"Oh sure. There's a giant pile of bones just through that tunnel. Second archway on the left."

Bill's eyebrows went up.

"Ha! Gotcha." Wendy laughed. "As far as I know she mostly goes for coyotes and jackrabbits."

"And when she squeaks and chitters and all that, do you understand what she's saying?" Bill asked.

"I understand what she means, but it isn't like a secret language as far as I can tell. What's with the third degree?"

"No third degree," Bill said, trying and failing to be casual. "Just curious. It isn't every day you meet a chupacabra."

CHAPTER 8
TOP SIDE

Ox and Rail were lying in bed watching a cheesy SyFy movie. The Slee-Z Motel might not have had much by way of amenities, but every motel in America had cable. The plot was thin and Ox was only half paying attention, so she heard right away when a new car pulled into the parking lot.

She sprung up to see what was happening.

"Get dressed, get dressed," she said, running to the bathroom. She threw Rail's clothes at him and shoved her limbs into her own.

"What's going on?" he asked, sliding his skin and bone legs into his pants.

"Stoney's here. And she brought that big guy . . . what's his name . . . Steve. Who calls themselves Steve? That's a cat's name." She ran back across the room and looked out the window again. "And he has a baseball bat. Great."

"Fuck man," Rail whined. "What do we do?"

"We give them back their shit, that's what we do."

Ox picked up a grease-stained paper bag from the floor. She opened a dilapidated dresser drawer and scooped a small mound of crumpled bills and shroom-filled ziplocs into the bag.

"Dude," Rail said. "Do we have to?"

There was a knock at the door, followed quickly by another one.

"Come outside with me," Ox whispered to Rail. "Better if this shit goes down in public. Stay close."

Rail begrudgingly got off the bed.

Ox opened the door and shoved her way outside, forcing the paper bag into the hands of an overweight white woman in a tie-dyed muumuu.

"Here's your shit. We're sorry. Just take it and go," she said.

Ox's push had driven them out from under the cover of the walkway. The four of them were standing on the asphalt now, next to the long gold two-door sedan Stoney and Steve had arrived in. The rain had mellowed to a drizzle.

"I don't know, kids," Stoney said. "What kind of message would that send? I run a clean camp, but only because everybody knows I don't put up with this kind of nonsense."

"Please, just let it go," Ox said. "Just this one time? Nobody will know, and you'll never see us again."

Stoney pressed her lips together and shook her head slowly. "No, I don't think that's how this is going to work. Steve," she said to the big guy, "you go ahead and do your thing now."

What happened next happened fast. Steve lifted the metal bat like a pitch was coming. He aimed for Ox's strike zone. But before he could swing, she sprang forward, grabbed the bat, and smashed the big oaf across the knees with it. He stumbled backward, running into the car.

"Hey now!" Stoney said. "Watch the paint on the Volaré. They don't make that color anymore!"

Ox stood ready to swing again, but Steve was not getting up. He sat sprawled on the wet pavement with his legs angled out in front of him. He was staring at his knees and scream-sobbing.

"Damn," Ox heard from behind her. "Check out what you did to the bat," Rail said.

She looked. The bat was curved now and had two concave humps where she'd hit Steve's knees. There was no way his kneecaps weren't shattered.

"Oh shit," she said. "I didn't mean to break your legs. I'm sorry, man. But still," she switched her focus to Stoney, "I think you guys better go." She took a step toward the hippie matron, flinching the bat like she might use it again.

Stoney, visibly shaken by Ox's extreme show of force, opened the expansive car door and dragged the weeping Steve into his seat. Then she quick-walked to the other side, saying, "We better not see you around here again. You come back and . . . and . . . well, you just better not come back."

She got behind the wheel and started the car.

At that moment, Ox and Rail heard someone yelling: "Hey! Hey! Stop them!"

They turned toward the sound. It was Shiva. He and a guy completely covered in curly black hair were running toward them from the direction of the well. Ox thought fast and jumped in front of the Volaré, which had already reversed out of the parking spot. She saw Stoney move the shifter on the steering column into drive.

The small girl waved her arms and yelled, "Stop! These people need help!" But Stoney hit the gas and steered around her, clipping the bumper of the Main Event Sideshow van. The four of them watched as the giant gold Plymouth sped out into the night.

"Damn it," Shiva said. "Think they'll come back?"

"No way," Ox said. "I'm so sorry, man. It didn't even occur to me to get their car for your friends. How are they?"

Shiva didn't answer. Instead, he screamed one long indiscriminate syllable. It wasn't exactly "Fuck," and it wasn't exactly not "Fuck." What was for sure about it was that it was loud and angry.

"Fuuuuuuuuaaarghkkk!"

He took a breath, stood up taller, and appeared to get his shit together.

"Okay," he said. "Is your cell phone charged?"

"I don't know."

Ox led them back into Room 7.

"Here it is," she said, picking up the phone from the nightstand. "It says it's charged but there aren't any bars."

Shiva took it from her and checked it for himself.

"Fuck," he said, clearly this time. "Fuck," he said again, throwing the phone to the floor. "Fuck, fuck, fuck," he said, stomping on the phone with every fuck.

He plunked down on the bed, hands on his knees and on his thighs, gaze on the floor.

"Sorry about the phone," he said. "I guess you were right, Dogface." He lifted his head to look toward the closed door, where he thought Dogface was. "It's a total dead zone."

There was no Dogface there.

"Where did he go?" Shiva asked. He jumped up and threw open the door.

"Maybe he went to get something from his room?" Ox suggested.

"No lights," Shiva said, pointing across the parking lot, then at all the rest of the rooms. "No lights anywhere but here. Shit. Argh." He leaned on the doorframe, letting his head knock against it. "I can't deal with this much longer. I feel like I'm losing my mind."

Ox and Rail looked at each other. Rail shrugged.

"Okay," Ox said. "We can help. I can help. What needs to happen?"

Shiva took a deep breath, collecting himself again. "There's a first aid kit in the back of that car." He pointed to the white Chevy in front of Room 10. "Me and Dogface are supposed to get it and take it to Jackie back down in the well."

"Why in the well?"

"Because of what happened to Hannah and to Kitten."

"Kitten?"

"My boss. The women who run this place killed her. They killed Hannah, too."

"What?! Why would they do that?" Ox asked.

"Because we're freaks."

"What the fuck?" Rail said.

Shiva didn't say any more. He just shook his head in a way that meant, "It's too fucking crazy for words."

"Okay, okay." Ox was even more energized by this new information. "We, or I, can get the kit and get it down the well. Then we'll find your friend, the hairy one. Do you have the keys to the car?"

"Yeah," Shiva said, digging Bill's keys from his pants pocket.

"You wanna wait here?" Ox asked.

"No. Nobody goes anywhere alone."

So the three of them left Room 7 and headed for the car. Shiva used the key to open the trunk. Sitting on the scratchy gray lining were three cases. One looked like a large tackle box, except it was red with a white cross on it. One was a gunmetal gray briefcase. And one was a long black case with a handle.

"There's a gun in that one, isn't there?" Ox said, pointing to the long one.

Shiva tried to unlatch it, but it had a combination lock. The briefcase, however, popped right open.

"Let's take all this inside," he said, tilting his head toward Bill's room, Room 10. "I want to look at this stuff for a minute."

Virginia had just finished setting up the kitchen the way Leslie told her to. She'd moved the table and chairs out of the way and put down the blue tarp they kept behind the seat in the pickup.

"Should I cover the counters and whatnot?" she asked.

"No. That'd be a waste of time. Blood's all going to run straight down on this one."

"Can't you just do it outside? It'd be so much easier to clean up outside."

"No, we can't do it outside," Leslie said, more condescending than usual. "Somebody might see us."

"Fine," Virginia said. "But if it gets messy, I'm not the one who's cleaning it up."

She was still debating covering at least the counters with sheets when Leslie brought the furry fellow in at gunpoint and had him undress. Virginia folded his clothes and set them in a pile just off the tarp. She laid his gun and bullets on the counter.

"Sit," Leslie said, swinging one of their marigold-yellow padded chairs to the center of the tarp.

"Wait!" Virginia said. She placed a tea towel on the seat of the chair. It was decorated with a cross-stitched yellow bird on a brown branch with green leaves. It matched the chair exactly. Virginia sighed at the sacrifice, but at least his backside wouldn't be directly touching the chair where she would have to eat breakfast tomorrow morning. "Okay, go ahead," she said.

Leslie motioned with her gun for Dogface to sit, and he did.

"What the fuck? We haven't done shit to you. Why are you doing this?" Dogface said. Panic made his words come fast.

Leslie stood in front of him with the gun aimed at his head while Virginia snaked a rope through the back of the chair and around his wrists and ankles.

"Hurry up," Leslie said.

"What? Nothing? You fucking cunts. You fucking shit fucking ass fucking cumbag fucking cunts. I get no kind of explanation about why you're tying me to a chair, why you're holding a gun on me? Why you killed my fucking friends?"

Leslie continued to ignore him.

"We're all good here," Virginia said, standing up and dusting her hands off on her jeans.

"Are you going to do to me like you did to Kitten, to Hannah?"

Leslie couldn't resist.

"Not exactly," she said. "You got something different wrong with you. You need a shave."

She put the gun down and picked up a straight razor, which she opened and brought right up close to Dogface's eyes, making a show of turning it this way and that, letting the overhead light glint off its blade.

"Get away from me! Fuck off! Stop!" His yells turned to screams as Leslie cut in, scoring the skin under his eyes and around his nose.

Leslie put a hand over his mouth to stifle his screams, but terror like that would find an outlet. Dogface started shaking and rocking in the chair.

"Hold him still," Leslie said to Virginia, who hugged him around the shoulders.

Leslie continued with her task. Using the razor, she traced the circumference of his face, creating a red line that bled like a soaker hose.

Every muscle in Dogface's body was taut. Noise came from his throat and Virginia struggled to keep him still.

Finally, starting at the top of his forehead, Leslie used the length of the razor to peel the skin from his frontal bone as if it were an apple. And once she had a flap of skin large enough to take hold of, she gripped it with both hands and yanked down, hard, shredding every single nerve ending in his face.

Dogface passed out.

"Well shit," Leslie said, standing there with his furry face in her hands.

"You were right about the blood," Virginia said. "It's all going straight down, just like you said."

CHAPTER 9
CHRISTOPHER

Jackie levered herself up with the help of a cane. She was done waiting. As she headed toward the cave exit, Bill said "Hey now, where do you think you're going?"

"I'm late for my appointment at the hotel spa. I've already missed my facial but if I hurry, I might still make the massage." She said it without stopping, without even looking at him.

"You can't go up there," Wendy said, chasing her. "You wouldn't stand a chance!"

Jackie turned abruptly as Wendy caught up to her. They were nose to nose.

"And I have a better chance down here? With you? With that?" She pointed at the neurotic chupacabra who was pacing the cave again. "If this thing in my side isn't already infected by—oh, I don't know—these sheets that were sandwiched between a bug-infested mattress and a sperm-covered comforter, or by being down in this mud hole, then that will be a full blown miracle—a miracle that would be for nothing if I don't change this bandage soon, since the blood and ooze leaking out of the burn is drying, and if I let it dry, then when I do finally get to change it, it's going to tear the wound back open and I will be back at square one, which was unbelievable pain. So, like it or not, I am going back up there, taking my chances with your homicidal crazy ladies, and finding a way to clean and cover this gaping hole in my side. And hell, if what you say about them is true, I don't have anything to worry about because, thanks to you, I am not a freak anymore!"

Wendy spoke quietly, cautiously. "But, I told you they've killed people just because they saw me, and . . . they don't like black people either." She tilted her head down and backed away. Whether she did this because she was embarrassed to have mentioned racism or because she was afraid of Jackie's next tirade, Jackie couldn't tell. Either way, it gave Bill a chance to step into the conversation.

"I'll help you," he said. "There's stuff for burns in my kit. Those guys should have been back by now. If something happened to them, then the longer we're down here, the sooner we become sitting ducks."

The little motel room was crowded. Jackie, Bill, and Wendy had just come in, and Shiva, Ox, and Rail were around the far bed, which was spread with papers and photos. Mostly photos.

There was a thump above them, as if a pterodactyl had landed on the roof.

"That's just my mom," Wendy said. "I think she's worried about me."

"Ya think?" Jackie said.

"So Bill," Shiva said, "you wanna explain any of this?"

Bill sat heavily on the unoccupied bed. "I told you I was here to kill myself. There's why."

Jackie and Wendy stepped closer to the others so they could see what everyone was talking about. The papers looked official, and the photos were surveillance shots of dozens of different people. A smaller, fanned-out stack of pictures was of animals, but not the kind of animals any of them had ever seen before.

"Let's hear it, man," Shiva said. "Because from where I'm standing, it's looking bad."

"It is bad. I killed them. I killed all of them."

"I think we're going to need the long version," Jackie said.

Bill sighed. "I was in Iraq, 24th Infantry Division—a sniper in a scout platoon. Every single person I shot at, I hit. The FBI got hold of my kill count and recruited me. Those people," he nodded toward the photos, "they were all considered threats to national security. I wasn't supposed to keep the pictures, but I did."

"No way. I call bullshit," Jackie said. "If somebody was running around assassinating that many people, it would have been on the news."

"There was always a cover crime," Bill said. "They'd get caught in the crossfire at a liquor store holdup or gunned down by a mugger in a park. I watched every one of those people go about their lives for days, sometimes weeks, coming up with the most believable scenario. I could tell you intimate details about every single one of them. That guy there resented taking his kid to taekwondo. And that one, she moonlit as a cam girl to pay for her baby sister's college."

"What about these?" Wendy asked, picking up the animal photos.

"I tried to quit. Really, I did. Several times. But they wouldn't let me. So I tried to miss, but I couldn't. I'd aim at something else instead—a bird, a tree. But I always killed the target. Eventually I just lost it. Wigged out. Even then, they wouldn't let me go. They just gave me a few counseling sessions and a transfer to cryptids."

"Cryptids?" Jackie asked. "Why does the government care about cryptids?"

"Alien DNA," he said. After the night they'd had, no one had the energy to question this. They all just took it in stride. Bill went on. "At first I was glad. I thought it would be like hunting, not murder, right? But it wasn't long before I realized that the reason cryptids are so good at hiding is because they're smart. So smart, sometimes they get their wires crossed." Bill pointed to the roof. "But still, even deep in a forest or out on a Zodiac in the middle of the ocean, what I hunted, I hit. So, on this mission, I decided to aim for me."

"This mission?" Wendy questioned. "She's your mission, isn't she? You're here to kill my mom."

Bill nodded. "Please believe me. I didn't mean to find her."

"And this," Shiva asked, picking up the long, black case and swinging it onto the bed, "I assume this is your rifle?"

"Yes."

"Good. Open it. You're going to cover me while I run to the trailer to get the knives. We need weapons."

"What?" Wendy said. "No! Didn't you hear him? He'll kill my mom even if he doesn't mean to. He can't go anywhere near that gun."

Ox spoke up. "I can do it. I've fired a rifle before. Probably not like this one, but how hard can it be?"

"I can guide you through it, if you want," Bill said.

"I'm okay with that," Shiva said. "Jackie?"

"Yeah, fine. But you can't go out there alone. Nobody goes anywhere alone. Plus there are two rolls," she said, referring to the way the knives and machetes were stored in the pockets of rolled-up lengths of canvas. "It would be better if two people went, in case you need to defend yourselves."

Wendy stepped forward. "I'll go. I'm strong. I'm fast. I can do it."

Jackie rolled her eyes at the Lizard Woman's eagerness. "Right. Whatever," she said. "But first, somebody's gotta help me with this." She lifted her black tank top to show the massive amount of blood that had seeped out from the wound in her side, the dark red stain on the makeshift bedsheet bandages nearly blending in with her dark skin.

It was Bill's turn to volunteer. "I got that. Where's my kit?"

Jackie sat on the closed toilet.

Bill unwrapped the little soap on the sink and thoroughly scrubbed his hands and forearms. He dried them on a scratchy hand towel and then tore open a small packet and pulled out an alcohol wipe, which he ran over every inch of his skin up to his elbows.

"You want morphine?" he asked her, tilting his head toward the floor where his open first aid kit sat, the top compartments spread out to reveal an abundance of medical supplies. "I would for what we're about to do."

"No," she said. "I can't afford to be fucked up right now. Let's just get this done."

Jackie winced as she lifted the hem of her shirt, folding the bottom half over top. Bill knelt down in front of her and used a pair of scissors that bent in the middle to cut through the layers of sheet.

"You shouldn't be so hard on her," he said.

She gave him a look that said, "Seriously? You want to talk about that now?"

He went on. "You're one of the very first people she's ever met. She wasn't even sure she was human until tonight. Hold this here." He placed her hand on the sheet strips crossing her stomach. "Can you turn sideways?" She rotated so the worst of it was toward him.

He slowly lifted the band of material across her back. When he got to the wound, it stuck.

"I'm going to have to get it wet to keep it from tearing open. Can you lean back?"

Jackie tilted back and rested her head against the peach and turquoise patterned wallpaper. Bill placed a towel on the floor underneath her and unwrapped one of the motel's flimsy plastic cups, which he used to ladle water over the bandage. Jackie grimaced but said nothing until he was done and the crusty strips of hotel sheet lay piled in the corner.

The wound was a raw, red hole in her side, textured with blackened chunks of charred flesh and the glistening clear ooze of lymph fluid.

"And who the fuck are you to tell me how to treat the person who killed my sister?" The sting of the air on her exposed flesh put malice in her words.

"Nobody. Just a sad old man with far too many kills to his name. Hers, at least, was an accident. You can't deny that," he said. And then, "I'm going to run some more water over this to clean it. You really need a hospital though. You're going to need a skin graft."

"It *was* an accident," Jackie said, baring her teeth and willing herself to stay still as the water flowed over her wound, thankful for the nerve endings that were burnt and therefore deadened. "But she killed my sister. My conjoined sister. You can't even begin to know what that means. Nobody can."

"No, I can't. But I do know what it means to regret killing someone, to have taken a life and wished like anything that you hadn't. Regret like that is its own kind of killer. Surely you've done something you regret. Surely you can empathize with her on that." He put the cup down and rifled through his kit.

Christopher, Jackie thought.

"All I'm going to say," Bill said as he found what he was looking for and ripped open the paper envelope, "is I think she deserves a second chance. She lives in a well and was raised by a chupacabra and cable TV for God's sake." He removed a clear, squishy sheet from the package. "Hydrogel. It'll keep it from getting dried out."

Jackie looked at Bill while he placed the new, space-age-looking bandage across her charred and oozing side. "A second chance. That's what Maddie would have said."

Finding love, for conjoined twins, is notoriously difficult. Chang and Eng, the original Siamese twins, had the best track record, but their situation still wasn't perfect. They married sisters who ended up hating each other. Their solution was to maintain separate households and switch from one family to the other every three days. And families there were. Between them, they fathered twenty-one children.

But female conjoined twins haven't been so lucky. Millie-Christine McKoy, the 19th-century slave girls who traveled the sideshow circuit as the Two-Headed Nightingale, were told from a young age that, while physically possible, sex for them would be so morally objectionable that marriage was simply not an option.

And then there were Daisy and Violet Hilton, who found fame in Vaudeville and, briefly, in Hollywood but never succeeded in love. Violet and her beau were refused a marriage license in twenty-one states on the grounds that the relationship was polygamous because Daisy was always present. Later, both sisters married for publicity stunts, but both of their "husbands" were gay. One marriage lasted ten years on paper, the other ten days.

Regardless of how impossible the dream, love was all Maddie really wanted. She was a romantic, whereas Jackie saw herself as a realist and was automatically suspicious of any boy who looked their way. Those who did were few and far between, so there was never really a problem. Until Christopher.

Christopher showed up their senior year of high school. He had come to help his grandma in her old age, he said. More like somebody couldn't wait to get rid of him, Jackie thought.

Right away he took a shine to Maddie. And he was just her type: tall, skinny, slightly bookish with his black-rimmed glasses.

Against Jackie's better judgment, Maddie and Christopher began seeing each other. Many nights were spent sitting on their couch, the three of them, watching a show, and then Jackie tuning out, putting in her earbuds, scrolling through her phone, ignoring the sweet talk and giggles going on beside her.

Maddie was flush with puppy love. Jackie experienced the hormones through their shared blood supply, but not the sweet and dreamy thoughts. She didn't trust Christopher as far as she could throw him, and without Maddie's help, that wouldn't be very far at all.

"Isn't he great?" Maddie said. "I didn't think I'd ever find a boyfriend, let alone one like him. Really, isn't it just amazing?"

Jackie smiled and redirected. "Quit mooning over him and help me with these dishes."

As things progressed between the couple, Jackie's suspicions of Christopher only grew deeper. At times, when Maddie wasn't paying attention, Jackie would swear he was looking at her, a shady gleam in his eye, as if asking her to conspire with him.

Then they went to prom. Maddie had never been so excited. Jackie's date was D'Quan, a long-time family friend who everybody knew was waiting until he left their small town to come out of the closet.

They did the whole shebang: dresses and up-dos and heels, dinner and pictures and dancing, and after, half-frozen metallic sleeves of strawberry daiquiris in a hotel room.

After one drink, D'Quan said, "Right. I'm going home."

"No! Please?" Jackie said, coming as close to begging as she ever had in her life.

"Yeah, I got stuff to do. You guys have fun."

"Shit," Jackie said under her breath.

"It's okay," Christopher told her. "We can have a good time, just the three of us." And he handed her another cold metal envelope of booze.

"Great. Sure. You guys go ahead," she said, putting in her earbuds.

Before long, Maddie and Christopher were petting heavily. Jackie tried to cut herself off from them, to give Maddie space, and for a while it worked. Then she felt a hand on her thigh. It was Christopher's. She placed it back on Maddie's leg, where she assumed it had strayed from. He put it back on Jackie, continuing to make out with her sister. Jackie moved his hand again and slid her leg as far away as she could.

He groped her breast.

Jackie stood up suddenly, bringing Maddie with her.

"We're leaving!" she said.

"No!" Maddie cried. "What is wrong with you? Why can't you let me have this?"

"He put his hand on my boob, Maddie!"

"It was a mistake," Christopher said to his girlfriend, "an honest mistake. They are awfully close together."

"There," Maddie said. "See, he apologized. Can you get over yourself, please, for once, and let me have this night?"

Jackie had heard that love can make you blind. Her sister must have been deeply in love.

"Ugh, fine. But one more slip and, I'm telling you . . ."

Christopher smiled. He moved to the head of the bed and patted the space next to him. Maddie, and therefore Jackie, scooched up to fill it.

Jackie turned up her music and angled herself as far away as she could. A few minutes of wet, slurping, teenage kisses later, Christopher moved down the bed and under the skirt of Maddie's dress. She lifted her hips and he rolled her pantyhose down her legs and off her feet. Then he got to work. Maddie's head tilted back and she closed her eyes, reveling in the new sensations.

Jackie felt a hand between her legs. Before she could respond, it stroked her labia through her stockings.

"Nope!" Jackie said, startling Maddie from her ecstasy. "Fuck this. We are leaving."

There was a struggle. Maddie tried to hold on to the headboard, but Jackie was stronger.

"And if you ever come around us again," Jackie said to Christopher while gathering their things, "I will ruin you."

"I'm sorry," Maddie said to him, crying. "I'm so sorry."

On that night, Jackie knew she was doing the right thing. But Maddie had seen it differently.

"Why couldn't you just go along with it? When are we ever going to have a chance like that again?"

"Perverts are everywhere," Jackie had said.

"But he loves me."

"He's just a pervert willing to put in the work."

Maddie was quiet then. She was quiet for weeks. A few times during that stretch when Maddie wasn't talking to her, Jackie wondered if she'd made a mistake. Was it really a sense of outrage that made her drag her sister out of that hotel room? Or was it inexperience and fear?

And now that Maddie was gone, she questioned it again. Had she denied her sister her only opportunity to experience one of life's greatest pleasures, or had she saved them both from a sexual predator?

The only thing she knew for sure was that nothing was ever simple for a freak.

CHAPTER 10
SHIVA'S ARMS

"There they are. They're making for the trailer, just like you said they would."

Virginia and Leslie were in the front office. Their apartment was starting to smell, and they weren't ready to clean it yet.

"Should I go back and get the kid's gun?" Virginia asked.

"No, I'm the only one who needs a gun. You're going to grab the female. I'll take care of the guy."

By the time Leslie was done dictating the plan, the two freaks had disappeared behind the trailer at the front of the building.

"Come on," Leslie said, and the women went out the front door. Immediately, one of the windows behind them shattered. Silent bullets flew through the dark from across the courtyard. Virginia sped up as Leslie's gun banged out three loud shots in a row. Glass broke again, but this time it wasn't near them.

Both women ran to the far end of the trailer. As they turned the corner, they caught the bald, scab-covered woman by surprise. Her eyes grew terrified.

"Shiva! Watch out!" she yelled, as she failed to catch the black bag he threw down to her from the bed of the trailer.

Shiva? Virginia thought. *That wasn't the name he used checking in. What had it been? Anton, that was it. Anton something*

Italian, something that sounded like pasta. Spaghetti? Macaroni? Rigatoni? That was it: Anton Rigatoni.

"Stop!" Leslie yelled. "Get down from there," she said to the four-armed man, whatever his name was.

Shiva hopped down from the back of the trailer. Leslie kept the gun trained on him while Virginia begrudgingly took hold of the lizard freak's upper arms.

"Move it," Leslie said, pressing the barrel of the gun into Shiva's back. "We're going inside." She maneuvered so that as they turned the corner around the trailer and came into the line of sight of Room 10, he was in front of her. They had no shot.

Virginia followed, but before the women got their hostages to the covered walkway, there was an ear-piercing screech from above. Something just out of sight skittered and scraped across the top of the motel. Roofing shingles arced up and fell to the ground. A white blur, glowing against the night sky, jumped from the end of the building high into the air. It glided toward them, growing larger, all teeth and claws, aiming for Virginia.

"Shoot it, Leslie! Shoot it!" Virginia yelled, but there wasn't time.

As the animal's fangs clamped onto Virginia's shoulder, she let burst a terrified wail, and the scaly young woman from the well wrenched herself away, leaving Virginia with handfuls of dead skin. When the chupacabra saw that the Lizard Girl was free, she released the older lady and flew heavily up into the air, circling the scene. In full panic, Virginia pushed Leslie out of the way in her run for the door, wanting nothing other than to be deep inside the building.

As she ran back to Room 10, Wendy's arms were loaded down with both rolls of blades. She was checking over her shoulder so often, she stepped into the corner of the field of glass. While the sandals protected the sole of her foot from puncture wounds, she wasn't ready for the shifting surface, made worse by the recent rain. Her ankle rolled and the outside of her foot was bedazzled with blue and green shards.

She ran on.

When she got to the door it opened for her. She tripped into the room and threw her bundles on the bed.

"They got Shiva," she said, out of breath.

Wendy took in the disheveled state of the room. The sniper rifle was still set up: the barrel in the open half of the window, the bipod stand on the air conditioner, and the butt of the gun on the bed. As for the other half of the window, both panes were shattered. There was glass on the floor and the bed. The comforters of both beds had slid partway down, leaving garish-colored mounds of material on the floor. She saw that Bill had opened the door for her. Jackie was sitting against the wall on the far side of the dresser. Her face was blank. Completely blank.

"Where are Ox and Rail?" Wendy asked.

Bill nodded toward the space between the second bed and the bathroom wall. Wendy walked over slowly, not wanting to see what was there, but knowing she had to. Ox's crying face came into view first. Then Rail's lifeless body, his head resting in Ox's lap.

"He was shot?" Wendy said, feeling stupid for asking something so obvious.

"No," Bill said. "His heart gave out. His body couldn't handle the adrenaline."

Ox sniffled and swallowed her tears. "He said it could happen any time. I didn't believe him."

"Move him out of the way," Leslie told Virginia, pointing her chin toward Dogface, whose skin hung from his upper body like a sweatshirt tied around his waist.

"Leslie, that thing bit me! Look at it. It looks like my shoulder was caught in a goddamn bear trap!"

"Well boo-fucking-hoo. Are you going to help me with this or not? If we don't get this done tonight, there may not be a tomorrow for us."

Virginia wasn't sure what Leslie meant by that. No tomorrow because they'd be in jail? Because the freaks who were left would kill them? Or because, if Virginia didn't help, they would be over as a couple, Leslie would kick her out?

But the situation was urgent, so Virginia pitched in, the way Virginia always did. She slid the dead young man and his chair with its utterly ruined tea towel to the corner of the kitchen. She only caught the chair leg on his hairy hide once in the process.

"Lay down," Leslie said to Shiva.

"No," he said back at her.

She shot him in the shin.

He crumpled to the floor, mouth open with no sound coming out.

"I want this one spread eagle," she said to Virginia.

"Eagles don't have four wings."

"Do you always have to be a smart ass? Just grab his normal arms and put them above his head, will you?"

Virginia did as she was bid. Squatting down, she pushed Shiva back on the blue tarp, into the puddles of Dogface's congealed blood. He tried to fight her off, to pull his arms away, and Leslie shot him in his other shin. After that it was easier. He wasn't even screaming anymore.

His smaller arms flailed uselessly in the air.

Leslie set down the gun and picked up an ax that was leaning against the end of the cabinets.

When did she put that there? Virginia wondered.

With a great big smile, Leslie stepped on Shiva's little left hand, pinning his arm to the floor. She lifted the ax overhead and brought it down, severing the limb from its body. Blood squirted out of the new orifice. Close to the heart, it flew high into the air.

"Aw geez, Leslie. Look at that. It's on the coffee mugs and everything. That's just gross. You know what? I'm done here. I'm going to go clean up this bite and maybe take a shower."

"Fine. Suit yourself. I've got this."

Virginia dropped Shiva's arms, which fell with no resistance. As she walked away, she heard another thump and knew the four-armed man was no more.

CHAPTER 11
VIRGINIA'S DECISIONS

Jackie had seen a lot of unbelievable things over the last few hours, but this took the cake. One of the homicidal women, the granny-looking one, was walking across the courtyard toward their room.

"Bill," Jackie said. "Gun! Gun!"

He saw what she was talking about and hurried toward the rifle. But, because he was looking out of the window instead of where he was going, his foot caught in the slick pile of comforter on the floor at the end of the bed, which yanked the rest of the blanket toward him, which caused the butt of the gun to rotate off the bed and drop toward the floor. He reached out to catch it as he was falling forward and shot himself through the head.

There was a thump on the roof, followed by the whump-whump-whump of something heavy rolling down the pitch. Finally, a body—white and roughly wolf-sized—fell off the tin awning that covered the walkway in front of Room 10.

With one shot, he had taken out both of his targets.

Jackie and Ox looked at Wendy, who didn't say a word. Instead, her face became fierce, determined. She tossed Jackie the roll of Maddie's throwing knives and helped herself to two of Hannah's machetes.

"Dry your eyes, Ox," Wendy said as she handed the tiny Strong Woman a machete. "We'll cry later."

Ox wiped her face with her shirt and set her shoulders back. The three of them gripped their blade handles and waited.

Just below the window, where they could not help but see as they watched the killer's approach, the hole in Bill's head slid slowly down the shaft of his upright gun. Inching along, the barrel had to be filling with a plug of brains like a straw being pushed through jello. When the black metal tip finally connected with the inside of the back of his skull, both he and his rifle tilted to the side and fell against the air conditioner.

There was a knock at the door.

Jackie limped over and leaned against it. "What do you want?" she asked.

"To apologize," the woman said.

"Seriously?"

"Seriously."

"Are you armed?"

"No. I come in peace."

She checked with Ox and Wendy. Wendy brandished her machete. "Let her in."

Holding one of Maddie's pointed knives in the same hand as her cane, Jackie opened the door and hurried the woman inside.

"Her name's Virginia," Wendy said.

"Yes—" Virginia started to say, but Jackie interrupted her.

"Shut up. Sit down."

She did, on the second bed, as it was the nearest available non-glass and -blood and -brains covered surface. If she saw Rail's lifeless body between the bed and the wall, she didn't react to it.

Jackie and Wendy and Ox stood around her, weapons ready.

"Where are Dogface and Shiva?" Jackie asked.

"They're . . . dead," Virginia said. "I'm so sorry. Really, just so sorry."

"Was it an accident?" Jackie asked.

"No. It was Leslie."

"And did you try to stop her?"

"No," Virginia said, hanging her head.

"Did you help her?"

"I didn't hurt anybody," she said.

"Oh, nice deflection," Ox broke in. "Did you guys catch that? Let's just fucking kill her."

Jackie was a little surprised at this new side of Ox, but then again, she'd only known her for a couple of hours, and Ox had only just stood up from holding Rail's dead body for much longer than Jackie had expected her to.

"Hold on," Wendy said. "Isn't this the part in the movie where one of us says, 'We can't do that. Then we would be just as bad as they are?'"

"Yeah," Jackie said. "I don't give a shit about that. Do you?"

"Not really," Wendy said.

For a long moment they all leaned toward Virginia, blades first. The terror was plain on the older woman's face.

"Wait!" Jackie said, and the girls all rocked back on their heels. "We might be able to use her."

"Yes! Use me! What can I do for you?" Hope shined in Virginia's eyes.

"You can be my human shield," Jackie said.

The hope went out again.

Jackie told her sister freaks her plan.

Wendy and Ox ducked around the corner of the building and scurried up the trellis. Once inside the attic, Wendy didn't

111

bother replacing the vent cover. The Lizard Woman led the way, slinking through her old haunt in the dark. Ox followed less gracefully as she tried to negotiate the center beam with a long, curved metal shaft in one hand. They made their way to the manager's apartment, hoping to get the jump on Leslie.

"Let's go," Jackie said to Virginia. She had extricated the rifle from Bill's head; it dripped blood and brain matter as she motioned with it toward the door.

"What if she shoots me?"

"Then you'll be like everybody else around here tonight."

"You don't understand. I don't want her to have to live with having killed me."

"I'm beginning to see the problem here," Jackie said.

"What do you mean?"

"There really isn't time to explain. Open the door."

The rain had stopped and there was a fine mist rising as the water on the asphalt evaporated into the hot desert night. Limping along, leaning on the cane in her left hand and struggling to hold the long, heavy gun in her right, Jackie goaded Virginia past the dead chupacabra and around the field of broken glass. When they were almost across the courtyard, Leslie appeared at the office door. She held a pistol out in front of her.

"Don't shoot!" Virginia said.

"What in the hell are you doing, Ginny? How did you get yourself caught?"

"I was trying to apologize, to see if I couldn't make this whole thing go away."

"Featherbrain. Now how am I supposed to hit that black girl without shooting through you? She's so dark, I can hardly see her as it is." Leslie sighed. "Guess I'll just have to take my shot and see what happens."

Virginia closed her eyes and lifted her hands to protect herself, as if that would do any good. But the shot never came. When she peeked through her fingers, Ox and Wendy were standing over Leslie's prostrate body. Ox was holding a bent piece of metal, which used to be a baseball bat.

"Is she dead?" Jackie asked.

"Maybe," Ox said.

Wendy squatted down and checked for a pulse the way they always did on TV. "She's still alive."

The smell in the office was terrible. The closest thing to it Jackie had ever experienced was when a cat had died under their house. She didn't want to know why it smelled that way, but at the same time she needed to.

As she started behind the desk, Ox said, "You don't want to go back there."

"You're right," Jackie said and kept walking.

Wendy was leaning in close, analyzing her birth mother's face from just inches away, when Leslie started blinking.

"She's awake," Wendy called out.

The red-haired woman opened her eyes and found herself in her small kitchen, tied to a chair in the middle of the once-blue tarp. The tarp was now the color of cherry wood—a deep reddish-brown. Virginia was tied to another chair on her right.

The three young women positioned themselves in front of the killers, with Jackie in the center, Ox to her right, and Wendy on her left.

"So, what do you think?" Jackie said to Leslie. "Tied up by a black girl, an Asian, and your own freak daughter. Pretty ironic, isn't it?"

Leslie looked away, as if doing her best to pretend none of this was happening.

"How does it feel," Jackie went on, "to be responsible for so many deaths? I mean Kitten and Hannah and Dogface and Shiva, obviously." Her gaze fell on Dogface and Shiva's mutilated corpses and she almost lost her train of thought. But then she remembered Maddie and all the other bodies scattered around the motel grounds. "But the others are on you too, all because you couldn't treat Wendy like a human being."

Leslie's eyes flashed to the Lizard Woman at the name "Wendy."

"It's because of you that she was in the attic watching television and fell through the ceiling, killing Maddie. It's because of you that Rail overdosed on his own adrenaline during a gunfight that never should have happened. It's because of you that Virginia came charging over, making Bill trip onto his rifle, killing himself and Wendy's chupacabra foster mom."

Jackie paused, doing the math.

"That's eight deaths on your tab, just from tonight. How does that feel?"

Leslie continued to ignore her.

Ox leaned forward, spitting venom. "Why are you even talking to her? She's a monster. What are you hoping she'll say? That she's sorry?"

"I don't know," Jackie said. "I guess I'm looking for a reason not to kill her. Maddie said I was too impulsive. I mean, just because I want to kill somebody doesn't mean I should, right? I wanted to kill her earlier." She hitched a thumb at Wendy.

Wendy coughed politely. "Not to beat a dead horse, but I can't help but feel like one of us needs to point out that we've each lost the person most important to us tonight, and maybe we aren't quite in the right mindset for making life and death decisions."

"We each lost the one we were trying to protect," Jackie said. "And while it's too late for them, it's not too late for the next freaks or weirdos or Asians who might come by here."

"But we don't have to kill her to protect those people," Wendy said.

"Please?" Ox said. She might have meant, "Explain?" or she might have meant, "Oh, but can't we?" Wendy chose to believe the former.

"There's a truck. They wouldn't have disabled their own truck. I can't drive it, but maybe one of you two can. We can put them in the back and take them to the police."

"We could do that," Jackie said. "I can drive. Dad taught me but not Maddie because I was on the left. She was angry for months."

"Ugh," Ox said. "That would take so long."

"But at least we wouldn't be murderers," Wendy said.

"Fine," Ox agreed.

"Okay," Jackie said. "But how do we do it? How do we get them in the truck?"

"I can lift them in, chair and all, no problem," Ox volunteered.

"Wow. You're really useful to have around," Jackie said.

"Thanks," Ox said, her hardened face breaking into a small smile. "That means a lot to me."

During all of this banter, what the girls didn't see was that Virginia had found that, while she couldn't undo her own restraints, she was able to reach her fingers over and pick at Leslie's. Whenever the freaks looked away, whenever they spoke to each other, she made a little more progress, undid another knot, came a little bit closer, she hoped, to her own freedom.

And it was now, with the girls trading compliments, that Virginia undid the last knot in Leslie's ropes.

Leslie didn't hesitate. She stood from her chair, surprising all three girls, and lunged for the gun on the counter. But she slipped on the gore-covered tarp. Instinctively, she reached out for the nearest thing to keep herself from falling, and that nearest thing was Ox. Leslie was already well into her fall and ended up grabbing the girl around her knees.

Ox's legs slid out from under her. She fell back, hitting her head on the linoleum with a sickening thud. Blood pooled beneath her broken skull.

Wendy lost it.

Machete in hand, she went at her biological mother—thwack-thwack-thwack-thwack—and she didn't stop until the woman's torso was a red and meaty pulp, her clothes were in shreds, and all life was drained from her body.

When Wendy was finally done, she stood up and tossed the machete aside. She straightened her shirt and said, "Shall we go?"

And the two girls walked away—one leaning heavily on a cane and the other covered head to toe in blood spatter.

Virginia sat alone, surrounded by carnage and tied to her chair. She heard the girls find the keys to the truck in the office. She listened to the jingle of the bells on the door as they left the building. She heard the truck start up and drive away.

Jasper, who Leslie hadn't wanted to hire, would be in soon. He would untie her. Then what? Would he help her clean it all up? Would he want to go to the police? Could she convince them she was a victim? Would they let her keep the motel? If not, she had nowhere to go. Maybe it would be safer to add Jasper to the pile.

Virginia had a decision to make.

AMY M. VAUGHN is the author of *Skull Nuggets* (Bizarro Pulp Press) and the editor of the bizarro writing prompt compilation *Dog Doors to Outer Space* (Filthy Loot). She lives in Tucson, Arizona.

www.ingramcontent.com/pod-product-compliance
Lightning Source LLC
Chambersburg PA
CBHW071534100726
47908CB00004B/1393